The Extension of

Space in Globalization

The Extension of Space in Globalization

The Globally Extended Space and Human Rights in Theories and Modern and Contemporary Taiwanese and American Poetry

Sarah Yihsuan Tso

Sky Digital

Taichung, Taiwan   2020

The Extension of Space in Globalization: The Globally Extended
Space and Human Rights in Theories and Modern and
Contemporary Taiwanese and American Poetry / Sarah Yihsuan
Tso
The First Edition
Taichung City: Sky Digital Books
Publication Date: January 2020
Cover Size: 14.8 * 21 cm
ISBN: 978-957-9119-63-4 (paperback)

Issuer: Xiu-Meei Tsai
Author: Sarah Yihsuan Tso
Publication Date: January 2020
Purchase information:
Bank: Taiwan Cooperative Bank
Account Title: Sky Digital Books Co., Ltd.
Account No.: (006)-1070717-811498
Postal Account Title: Sky Digital Books Co., Ltd.
Postal Account No.: 22670142
List Price: 500 NT Dollars
E-book Patent No.: I-306564
Publisher: Sky Digital Books Co., Ltd.
Website: http://www.familysky.com.tw/
E-mail: familysky@familysky.com.tw

For my family and others

Contents

Acknowledgments

My university and myriad libraries across the world supported the writing of this book. My research assistants collected some of the research materials. I thank Wan-yu Lin for her biography in Chinese and Yin Ling for the interview. I am grateful to the National Science Council in Taiwan for a travel stipend. I thank as well anonymous reviewers for their comments, the publisher, and all other people who contributed to the creation of this book.

Chapter 1

Introduction

Globalization's impact on space has received prodigious critical attention, and I will give mine in this book. In this book, the extension of space is defined as the distension of space supranationally when space, beyond national territory, connects with physical space or cyberspace of another political entity, culture, or people. *The Extension of Space in Globalization: The Globally Extended Space and Human Rights in Theories and Modern and Contemporary Taiwanese and American Poetry* explores theories on space and theories on human rights in the globally extended space in Part I and canvasses modern and contemporary Taiwanese and American poetry on the globally extended space in Part II, citing theories and poetry, and commenting on cultures. This book raises large theoretical questions about the solely national and local definitions of space, human rights, and literature. In Chapter 2 and Chapter 3, Part I of this book, I argue that space and human rights, sites of contestation, are global-cum-local in various dimensions and are deterritorializing. I maintain in Chapters 4 to 6, Part II of this book, that modern and contemporary Taiwanese and American poetry illuminates the impacts of the globally extended space on freedom, the human mind, place, and poetics. Part II examines the poems expounding the globally extended space in globalization written by seven acclaimed major poets including Taiwanese poets Chou-yu Cheng, Wan-yu Lin, Hsiung Hung, Hsia Yu, and Yin Ling and American poets Jorie Graham and Bei Dao. Their poetry on the globally extended space commends sacrifices for freedom or chronicles its redefinitions. Their poetry reflects on an array of the extension's effects on the human mind including the intensification of solitude, the surfacing of the unconscious of the globetrotter, and nostalgia for territories, heritages, and space in childhood. And their poetry ponders global interrelatedness and its reverberations in poetics such as interconnectedness and openness.

In Part I, in addition to exploring current theories on space, I establish my own theories on space including the three dimensions of space (haecceitic dimension, social dimension, and social and international dimensions), two secondary dimensions (affective secondary dimension and virtual secondary dimension), and four descriptors for my three dimensions of space—heterogeneity in composition and deterritorialization for the haecceitic dimension, relatedness including the relation of space to time for the social dimension, and interrelatedness for the social and international dimension. Moreover, in my own theory on freedom in the globally extended space, I argue that freedom is ensured or transformed in the globally extended space. My theories and terms clarify the impacts of local-global interconnectedness on spatiality and on the nation-state's and people's reevaluations of human rights such as freedom.

In Part II, I maintain that modern and contemporary Taiwanese and American poetry on the globally extended space delves into the outcomes of the extension of space including the securing or redefinition of freedom and factors aggravating or assuaging solitude such as frauds, the commercialization of human relationships, and global travel. The poetry also probes the dominances of the unconscious and space of childhood during global travel and nostalgia for territories and heritages and for space in childhood. Moreover, modern and contemporary Taiwanese and American poetry chronicles people's fear about wars and global politics, the global interconnectedness among strangers, and interrelatedness. To explicate modern and contemporary Taiwanese and American poetry on the globally extended space, I coined my own literary terms including "the poetics of interrelatedness and openness" on interrelatedness, indeterminacy, and experimentality in Hsia Yu's poetry; "poetics of interrelatedness" on the self's interconnectedness with others in Graham's poetry; "prodigal place" on a place laced with other places and times; and the "othering of place" on the presence of the absent other at a place, the last two terms for Graham's poem "Event Horizon."

The book has seven chapters and is divided into two parts, "Theories on Space and Human Rights in the Global Era" and "The Extension of Space in Poetry." Part I, "Theories on Space and Human Rights in the Global Era," propounds my theories on space and on freedom in the globally extended space and explores current theories on space and on human rights in two theoretical chapters. Part II, "The Extension of Space in Poetry," examines the globally extended space in modern and contemporary Taiwanese and American poetry in another three chapters. Pronounced interconnections between Part I and II are commented on in Part II, whereas not all the theories in Part I are applied to the poetry in Part II.

This chapter, the introduction, advances my argument of the book and epitomizes its seven chapters. In Chapter 2, I maintain that space is multiscalar, deterritorialized, and multi-dimensional in current theories. In Chapter 2, my first contribution to theories on space is my conceptualization of the three dimensions of space—haecceitic, social, and social and international dimensions. Moreover, I argue that space has two secondary dimensions including its affective and virtual secondary dimensions. The affective secondary dimension is within the social dimension of space. The virtual secondary dimension belongs to the social and international dimension of space. My other contributions to spatial theories are my descriptors for my three dimensions of space. In my conceptualization, space in the haecceitic

dimension is heterogeneous in composition and deterritorializing. Relatedness is the descriptor of the social
dimension. Interrelatedness is the descriptor of the social
and international dimension of space.

In addition, most of the recent theories on people in
space deal with the haecceitic dimension of space and, in
my two descriptors, its heterogeneity in constitution and
deterritorialization. Moreover, recent literary theories on
space conceive space as ontological, cultural, and
deterritorialized. Furthermore, recent scholarship defines
globalization as changes and as its dimensions. The
current consensus among scholars, I suggest, defines
globalization in its two impacts or dimensions,
interrelatedness and interdependency.

In Chapter 3, I maintain that in the age of globalization, since no later than the 1980s, the extension of space safeguards or redefines human freedom. In the globally extended space, global politics and transnational and global institutions and organizations as well as national institutions and groups redefine freedom and its enactment. Human rights are local-cum-global values within the nation-state and in the globally extended space of global civil society because human rights are abstract values, national values, and international and global values in my three dimensions. To scholars, freedom, a human right, is an ethical value as it is a moral, legal, and political value in the globally extended space with a trove of discordant definitions (Frost 75-77; Moyn, *The Last* 226-27). Next, on the voices or movements countering or endorsing human rights, Chapter 3 suggests that human rights are not adversarial to nationalism in a nation-state, or to isolationism in the globally extended space. Ideologies or people object to human rights because in the globally extended space human rights flow with fewer barriers than politics and people as Manuel Castells and Zygmunt Bauman both contend (Bauman, "Media" 301). My analysis in Chapter 3 suggests that anti-globalization movements and ideologies can be neutral to human rights, defend human rights, or infringe human rights. Moreover, the topic of this book, globalization, is intersectional and inclusive as a field and an approach for innumerable scholars across disciplines.

The globally extended space and freedom in the globally extended space are also central themes in modern and contemporary Taiwanese and American poetry and will be treated in Part II of the book. Chapter 4, "Taiwanese Poetry on the Globally Extended Space: Freedom, Territoriality, Nostalgia for Space, Solitude, Global Travel, Interconnectedness, and Fear," examines poetry on the globally extended space in globalization published after the 1950s and written by Taiwanese poet Chou-yu Cheng and Taiwanese woman poet Wan-yu Lin as well as by other poets including Taiwanese women poets Hsiung Hung, Hsia Yu, and Yin Ling. These poets' agendas on the globally extended space include the valorization and transformation of freedom, territoriality and the borders of the nation-state, nostalgia for space, solitude, global travel, jet lag, space lag, global interconnectedness, and fear confronting wars and global politics. Chou-yu Cheng emblazons sacrifices for freedom on the globe and identifies three issues concerned with the territoriality of the nation-state in the globally extended space including sojourning, national security, and diaspora. He disapproves of border trespassing and delves into the nostalgia for national territories and for the heritages of culture and the Chinese language. Both Wan-yu Lin's and Hsia Yu's poetry on the globally extended space suggests that global interconnectedness is based on material conditions such as the Internet, capitalism, and global travel. In the first account, Wan-yu Lin's poetry suggests that modern people's loneliness intensifies because of impostures on the Internet and the commercialization of human relationships in both virtual and physical space. In the second, Wan-yu Lin's poetry suggests global travel as a remedy for this solitude to a certain extent. Hsia Yu's poetry in her book of poems *First Person* construes the global interconnectedness among strangers in a poetics of interrelatedness and openness, my coined term.

Taiwanese woman poet Hsiung Hung's poem "Writing a Poem in Jet Lag" dissects the dominance of the unconscious in jet lag and the ascendancy of the space of childhood in space lag for a globetrotter or a long-distance traveler, and defines nostalgia as pining for space of childhood. The poem "A White Dove Flew Over" written by Yin Ling commentates on the redefinition of freedom in the globally extended space more by global politics than by the nation-state and adumbrates that fear is people's cardinal emotion about wars and global politics in the globally extended space.

Moreover, the globally extended space is affective, deterritorializing, related, interrelated, and virtual in Taiwanese poetry's ideas of space examined in Chapter 4. For example, the globally extended space is affective in Chou-yu Cheng's poem "Celeste Sky." The globally extended space is deterritorializing in the poems written by Chou-yu Cheng, Wan-yu Lin, Hsia Yu, and Yin Ling. One of the two descriptors of my haecceitic spatial dimension also suggests that the globally extended space is deterritorializing. In Wan-yu Lin's poetry and Hsiung Hung's poem "Writing a Poem in Jet Lag," the globally extended space is related and affective. In addition, the globally extended space is interrelated and virtual in Wan-yu Lin's and Hsia Yu's poetry.

Furthermore, Chou-yu Cheng's poems "The Eternity of Václavské Square" and "You Did Not Return from the Trip" attest to my theory in the third chapter contending that the extension of space redefines or secures freedom. The poem "A White Dove Flew Over" written by Yin Ling corroborates my theory in Chapter 3 that human rights including freedom transform in the globally extended space, in the instances in this poem more by global politics than by nation-states. The poetry on freedom and human rights written by Chou-yu Cheng, Hsia Yu, and Yin Ling examined in Chapter 4 evokes all three of my dimensions of human rights as abstract values, national values, and international and global values.

Chapter 5, "Jorie Graham's Poetics of Interrelatedness," and Chapter 6, "Globalization and Universal Subjectivity in Bei Dao's 'Daydream,'" compare two American poets, Graham and Bei Dao, writing in English and Chinese respectively. I argue in Chapter 5 that in an acute awareness of others owing to the intensified global interconnectedness, Graham espouses a poetics of interrelatedness, my coined term. I maintain in Chapter 6 that Bei Dao's view of globalization illuminates the interrelatedness of literature. Bei Dao's poem "Daydream" advances a universal subjectivity in Johann Gottlieb Fichte's theory of free and rational human beings. Analyzed in Anthony Giddens's theory of trust, my term of the othering of place, and Fichte's theory of the relationship between the self and others, Graham's and Bei Dao's poetry testifies to literature's and our intercon-

17

nectedness in the globally extended space. The globally extended space is deterritorializing for Bei Dao and is interrelated for Graham. Human rights are abstract, international, and global values in Graham's poem "Event Horizon."

Chapter 7, the conclusion, revisits my argument about theories and literature on space and on freedom in the globally extended space. The last chapter explicates theories and terms on space and freedom in the globally extended space again and suggests future directions and agendas for research on space and globalization. One of the problematics already addressed by Chou-yu Cheng's poetry is that the distending of space globally does not prevail over state power in all instances or encompass all national territories.

Part I

Theories on Space and

Human Rights in the Global Era

Chapter 2

Multidimensional and Deterritorializing Space beyond the Nation-State: Theories on Space in the Global Era

Introduction

I argue that space in globalization is both local-global in myriad dimensions and deterritorializing. Current prominent theories on space examine space from "multiscalar," deterritorialized, and multi-dimensional stances (Masson 42; Susen 354). Most theories on people in space interpret the haecceitic dimension of space and the heterogeneity and deterritorialization of space. Like the theories on space in other disciplines, literary theories on space imagine space to be ontic, cultural, and deterritorialized.

My contributions to theories on space comprise three dimensions of space including the haecceitic, social, and social and international dimensions, my descriptors of my three dimensions of space, and two secondary dimensions of space including the affective and virtual secondary dimensions (see fig. 1). Space in the haecceitic dimension can be heterogeneous in composition and deterritorializing. Space is related in the social dimension and interrelated in the social and international dimension. Moreover, the affective secondary dimension of space belongs to the social dimension. My virtual secondary dimension is situated within the social and international dimension of space.

I will first define globalization and its two dimensions, interrelatedness and interdependency, before examining space in current theories and the purport of place and space. Scholars define globalization as dynamic changes or as its multiple dimensions. The recent consensus among scholars defines globalization as its two chief impacts, as well as its two dimensions: interrelatedness and interdependency.

Globalization Defined: Changes and Dimensions

Globalization is an overarching term in global studies to refer to the radical and dynamic changes in reality as well as concepts in ancient times and in what Giddens and other scholars call modernity. Globalization has multiple dimensions as scholars of global studies suggest. Yale H. Ferguson and Richard W. Mansbach maintain that globalization "*is a multidimensional phenomenon*" (288). A number of people define globalization by its multifarious economic, social, political, and cultural terrains. Recent scholarly consensus suggests that globalization can be portrayed by its impacts including, but not limited to, interrelatedness and interdependency as two dimensions of globalization.

For example, James R. Faulconbridge and Jonathan V. Beaverstock define globalization as interconnectedness through various types of flows (340). Faulconbridge and Beaverstock also maintain that interconnectedness is multiscalar, and as most scholars agree, unevenness and inequalities are two of the negative consequences of the status quo of globalization: "Globalization is not only about the interplays between local, regional, national and global scales, but also about interconnectedness, flows and uneven development in the world" (340).

Interconnectedness brings interdependency, and Robert O Keohane and Joseph S. Nye Jr., in another term "globalism," suggest that interdependency is one of the dimensions of globalization: "Globalism is a state of the world involving networks of interdependence at multicontinental distances" (105). Bauman maintains that of all forms of interdependency, economic interdependency is most salient:

> 'Globalization' means today no more (but no less either) than globality of our dependencies: no locality is free any longer to proceed with its own agenda without reckoning with the elusive and recondite 'global finances' and 'global markets', while everything done locally may have global effects, anticipated or not. ("Media" 301).

I will examine the causes of interconnectedness in the next section.

Interconnectedness in the Globally Extended Space, Technologies, and Neoliberalism

Interconnectedness in my view is the relational and affective dimensions of globalization apropos of a reality transformed by information and transportation technologies as well as neoliberalism (Castells, *Rise* 1). A primary dimension of globalization, the interconnectivity among people, nation-states, and the environment is an upshot of the extension of space owing to globalization in this age of netizens following the information revolution. In *The Rise of the Network Society*, Castells expatiates globalization from the perspective of information revolution and substantiates this theory of a society structured by the Internet with evidence from field research. This "Information Age" of netizens is also an age of travel and migration with plane tickets from low-cost airlines, tourism organized by budget travel agencies, wars among nation-states and militant groups, and uneven developments—the causality of the flow of ideas, news, capital as well as people (Castells, *End* 387). These flows increase and accelerate in globalization because of both the information revolution and neoliberalism as Peter A. Hall, Wade Jacoby, Jonah Levy, and Sophie Meunier suggest:

We use the term 'globalization' to refer to increases in the flows of people, goods, and capital across national borders, to the neoliberal ideas that have promoted those flows, and to the growth in transnational communication made possible by a revolution in information technology. (2)

Current Theories on Space in Globalization

Space is multiscalar, deterritorialized, and multidimensional in recent theories on space. I maintain that space has three dimensions including the haecceitic dimension, social dimension, and social and international dimension. In my formulation, space can be heterogeneous in composition and deterritorializing in its haecceitic dimension. Space is related in the social dimension, whereas it is interrelated in the social and international dimension. Moreover, I conceptualize two secondary dimensions—the affective secondary dimension within the social dimension and the virtual secondary dimension within the social and international dimension. Furthermore, recent theories on the relationship between space and people primarily expound the haecceitic dimension of space. In addition, literary theories on space envision space to be ontic, cultural, and deterritorialized.

I. Multiscalar Space

Recent feminist theories on space suggest that the women's movement is multiscalar in space globally. Dominique Masson remarks on the transnational local-global interconnections, sisterhood, and mutual support among the women's movement:

> Examining transnational organizing and action through a multiscalar, rather than a uniscalar, lens directs our attention toward exploring the linkages between the transnational and other scales of feminist and women's movement activity. (42)

The idea of multiscalar space is closely linked to deterritorialized and transforming space. The deterritorialized space will be elaborated in the following section.

II. Deterritorialized Space

Space for Gilles Deleuze and Félix Guattari is rhizomatic and anti-genealogical, and in this space people and objects are in a relational network in deterritorialization, a process often accompanied by reterritorialization (11). Like Deleuze and Guattari, on the notion of liquid modernity, Bauman interprets an uncertain and deterritorializing reality without a denouement:

> It is the *removal* of such 'final state' (or any finishing line for that matter) from the horizon of the 'modernizing' melting/liquefying bustle that sets apart the 'liquid' from the sketched above 'solid' phase of modernity. . . . In that new order, flexibility is the sole stability, transience the sole durability, temporary-ness the sole permanence, liquidity the only solidly attached quality of situations as much as of its authors/actors; all in all, *uncertainty is the only certainty.* ("'Liquid Modernity'" 394-95)

Likewise, in "women's social space," in Cunxiao Huang's view, "difference," a concept of deterritorializing differentiation, and "equality" are the two foci of current research (161). Research on women's space in the 1980s emphasizes the impact of "women's experience on landscape or" territory (Cunxiao Huang 24). The key concept of research in the 1990s and the twentieth century shifts to postmodernist "difference," Cunxiao Huang suggests (25).

III. Multi-dimensional Space

Doreen Massey, Nigel Thrift, and David Harvey's schemata of space explore the myriad dimensions of space in its relationship to society and language. To these dimensions, I add the affective and the virtual secondary dimensions, my three dimensions, and their descriptors (see fig. 1). To Massey, space has at least three dimensions, *"relationality," "multiplicity,"* and *"malleability"*:

> space is a product of interrelations (*relationality*), a physical realm composed of heterogeneous parts (*multiplicity*) and an open reality constantly under construction (*malleability*). (Susen 353)

Simon Susen summarizes six dimensions of space Thrift postulates including five social dimensions and a linguistic dimension. These dimensions to Susen are:

> (i) *Contingency*: Space is socially constructed. . . . (ii) *Temporality*: Space is situated in time, just as time is located in space. . . . (iii) *Agency*: Far from representing simply a social fact, space constitutes

also a social act. . . . (iv) *Intersubjectivity*: Even in a globalized environment, . . . interpersonal relations, established in communicatively structured lifeworlds, continue to be vital to the functional reproduction of the social fabric. (v) *Contextuality*: Notwithstanding the degree of planetary interconnectedness, critical geographers need to be sensitive to local and regional specificities. . . . (vi) *Discursivity*: Just as different spaces create different discourses, different discourses generate different spaces. (354)

Harvey maintains that there are three concepts of space and time—"absolute, relative, and relational"—and that "space is constituted by the integration of all these definitions" (134). "Absolute space is fixed and immovable," to Harvey (134). "Relative space ["spacetime"] is . . . the space of *processes and motions*. Space cannot here be understood separately from time" (Harvey 135). "The idea that processes produce their own space and time is fundamental to the relational conception," Harvey next explains (136). In this third mold, space and time are relational as the two orders coalesce: "Space and time are internalized within matter and process. . . . They fuse into spacetime" (137). Harvey also establishes the relationship among the three molds as dialectical: "the three conceptions of absolute, relative, and relational need to be held in dialectical tension with each other" (141).

Moreover, in my nomenclature, affective space refers to personal, familial, and communal space, and space in memory. Virtual space, the space of the Internet and in media, is simultaneously local and global. I argue that

Dimensions of Space in Theories					
Tso's three dimensions	*Tso's descriptors*	*Doreen Massey's three definitions*	*Nigel Thrift's six dimensions*	*David Harvey's three ways*	*Tso's secondary dimensions**
Haecceitic dimension	1. Heterogeneity in composition	Multiplicity			
	2. Deterritori-alization	Malleability			
Social dimension	1.-7. Relatedness				
	1.	Relationality	Contingency		
	2 to 4. Relationship to time		Temporality		
	2.			Absolute (place or physical space)	
	3.			Relative ("space-time")	
	4.			Relational ("spacetime")	
	5.		Agency		
	6.		Intersubjectivity		Affective
	7.		Discursivity		
Social and international dimension	Interrelatedness		Contextuality		Virtual

Fig. 1. Dimensions of Space in Theories.

*These are other secondary dimensions of space in my opinion.

there are three main dimensions of space in theories—haecceitic, social, and social and international dimensions. The first dimension of space, the haecceitic dimension, is a rubric for the definitions of space as its differentiating traits. Space in the haecceitic dimension is heterogeneous in composition and deterritorializing. Heterogeneity refers to the disparity of the constituting elements of space or Massey's definition of the multiplicity of space. Deterritorialization portrays the transformation of the notion of space or malleability in Massey's term.

My second dimension of space, the social dimension, comprises the connotations of space in society. The descriptor that corresponds with the social dimension in my view is relatedness. The social dimension includes Massey's definition of space as relationality and Thrift's five interpretations of space—"*Contingency,*" "*Temporality,*" "*Agency,*" "*Intersubjectivity,*" and "*Discursivity*" (Susen 354). The subcategory of relationship to time includes Thrift's dimension of "*Temporality*" and

Harvey's three ideas of space as "absolute, relative, and relational" (Susen 354; Harvey 141).

My first secondary dimension of space, space as affective, corresponds with Thrift's spatial dimension of intersubjectivity (Susen 354). My third dimension of space suggests that space in globalization is interrelated, linked, and extended globally. My social and international dimension corresponds with Thrift's dimension of contextuality. I also propose virtual space as a secondary dimension of my third social and international dimension.

IV. Space to People

Like the multiple and malleable space Massey explores, heterogeneity and deterritorialization are the current focal points in theories on space and people in issues at stake including transnational families, creolization, and diaspora. Scholarship is devoted more to families and communities than to individuals, a wry phenomenon given the surge of individualism in this century. Ulrich Beck and Elisabeth Beck-Gernsheim define "'world families' (or 'families at a distance', or 'global families')" as "people living in, or coming from, different countries or continents" in opposition to traditional "'one-nation families' (or 'close-knit families', or 'local families')" (15, 2). Creolization and diaspora intertwine in their significance and in reality in the view of Robin Cohen and Olivia Sheringham: "Creolization and diaspora need to dance together in a warm and intimate embrace, a 'creospora'" (158). The space occupied by humans in current theories is familial, cultural, and transforming while iconoclastic.

V. Space in Literary Theories

The paradigms in literary theories on space are consistent with those in theories on space in other disciplines. Milestone and recent literary theories on space examine space from the theoretical frameworks of ontology (haecceitic and social dimensions), culturalism (social dimension), and deterritorialization (haecceitic dimension). To Gaston Bachelard, poetry is an ontic art, and Bachelard contends that "the poetic image has an entity and a dynamism of its own; it is referable to a direct *ontology*" (xvi). Poetics of space for Hsiao Hsiao is "the unconscious inclinations of poets while they deploy space" (2) In their theories on space in literature, Yun-Wen Lin,

Paul Giles, Susan Manning, and Andrew Taylor all entertain culturalism. Yun-Wen Lin maintains that Taiwanese travel writings in the 1990s and the first decade of the twenty-first century portray an independent and integral self and its interactions with other cultures (33-34). Giles applies Samuel Hungtington's theory of the clashes among civilizations to literature: to Giles, "transnationalism seeks various points of intersection . . . where cultural conflict is lived out experientially" (65). Likewise, for Manning and Taylor, culturalism serves as common ground in recent literature when the imagery of the frontier is supplanted by the image of porous borders among cultures and cultural flows: "The image of the frontier . . . has been replaced by that of borders permeable to the reciprocal flow of cultures" (2). Furthermore, applying

Deleuze and Guattari's concept of the rhizome, Françoise Lionnet and Shu-mei Shih maintain that the articulation of "minor literature" has "network structures" (2).

Place vs. Space

In current theories, place is a much narrower concept than space. To John Agnew, in addition to the mundane understanding that place is a physical locale, place has two other dimensions including the subjective and the social (5-6). Place has three cognitive dimensions for Noel Castree:

1   *Place as location*—a specific point on the earth's surface.

2   *A sense of place*—the subjective feelings people

have about places, including the role of place in their individual and group identity.

3   *Place as locale*—a setting and scale for people's daily actions and interactions. (155)

In this book, unless otherwise indicated, the first definition of place applies whenever the term appears.

Conclusion

Recent scholarship conceptualizes space as "multiscalar," deterritorialized, and multifaceted (Masson 42; Susen 354). As my contributions to spatial theories, my conceptualization proposes haecceitic, social, and social and international as the three dimensions of space and the affective and virtual as two secondary dimensions of space.

My two descriptors for my haecceitic dimension portray space as heterogeneous in composition and deterritorializing. My descriptor for my social dimension of space, relatedness, includes a secondary descriptor on the relationship of space to time. My descriptor of interrelatedness for my third social and international dimension of space accounts for the extended space in globalization. A secondary virtual dimension of space is within the social and international dimension. To most scholars, globalization, the larger context of this book, is a term for dynamic changes or the many dimensions of globalization. In recent years, the majority of scholars define globalization as its two primary impacts or two dimensions, interrelatedness and interdependency. Moreover, recent spatial theories on space and people explore mostly the haecceitic dimension and the heterogeneity and deterritorialization of space, in the terms of my first dimension of space and two descriptors of this dimension, respectively. Space is imagined as ontological, cultural, and deterritorialized in recent literary theories on space. In the next chapter, I will examine recent theories on human rights in extended space.

Chapter 3

National and Global Values: Theorizations of Human Rights in the Globally Extended Space

Introduction

Like space, human rights in the global era in recent
theories are local-global, multidimensional, and deterritorializing. I maintain that in our era of globalization, since
at least the 1980s, the extension of space to a certain
degree ensures or redefines human rights such as freedom.
This chapter examines recent theories on human rights in
the globally extended space in globalization in four
sections and suggests that when space is extended, the
significance and practice of freedom are in flux and are
transformed by transnational and global institutions and
organizations as well as global politics, not defined
entirely by national institutions and groups. The insti-

tutions and publics within a nation-state with power to define and defend human rights such as freedom are the state, the local culture including customs and legacy, the local society, and the local community. The institutions and groups with power to promote the currently recognized value of human rights including freedom supranationally comprise the Internet, global media, capitalism, INGOs, NGOs, the UN, IMF, WTO, and other transnational or global political, economic, or professional institutions. Section I, "Human Rights in the Globally Extended Space and Their Cosmopolitanization," suggests that human rights are not just local values. Human rights are global values as the space of human rights transforms and deterritorializes in globalization. Section II, "Human Rights' Dimensions," states the reasons for the reconceptualization and deterritorialization of human rights by explicating that human rights are abstract values, national values, and international and global values in their three dimensions. Freedom in the globally extended space is an ethical value as much as it is a moral, legal, and political value because it could have conflicting interpretations within and beyond a nation-state (Frost 75-77; Moyn, *The Last* 226-27). Section III, "Human Rights within the Nation-State and Globally: Not Antagonistic to Nationalism or Isolationism," examines oppugnancies to human rights within the nation-state and globally. Section III suggests that human rights are not inimical to nationalism within the nation state, or to isolationism in the international arena. Some people dispute human rights because human rights flow more smoothly in the globally extended space than politics and people. In section IV, "Human Rights and Anti-globalization," I suggest that anti-globalization movements and ideologies can remain neutral toward, protect, or encroach on human rights. Finally, owing to its intersectionality and inclusiveness, globalization is a field and an approach of the globally extended space of many scholars and scientists in the humanities and sciences. Human rights, including freedom, are local-cum-global values and are simultaneously local values within the nation-state and global values in the globally extended space of global civil society.

Human Rights, including Freedom, in Globalization

Stefan-Ludwig Hoffmann explains the dilemma of human rights in this and the past century, in which the lack of law enforcement for human rights violations exists alongside the movements to stop human rights abuses (25). The extension of space leads to the possibility of shared global values such as human rights, freedom, and suffrage following the definitions of liberal states. While these values rest on the works of modern Western thinkers, customs and tradition pertaining to one's communal, civic, and gender roles and their collateral, relevant responsibilities and obligations, occlude homogenous definitions of human rights globally. However, confronting the reality of this extension of space, at least to a certain degree people as well as governments within a nation-state are impelled to tailor domestic policies and traditional views to a global standard of human rights. This chapter examines current examples of this emerging global standard and suggests that global values and global civil society are two products of this extension. This chapter explores human rights as examples of the global values that extend throughout most of the terrains of the world. Global values have spread over a wider expanse of the world as activities of global civil society disseminate from industrialized countries to developing and underdeveloped parts of the world over recent years. Paolo Gerbaudo and Mario Pianta's study on the diffusion of values corroborates that from 1990 to 2008, concentration of the events of global civil society "in Europe and North

America" dropped significantly—from less than two-thirds to "more than one-third" of all occurrences (Kaldor, Moore, and Selchow 191).

I. *Human Rights in the Globally*
   Extended Space and Their Cosmopolitanization

Human rights are more than local values within the nation-state. The space of human rights metamorphoses and deterritorializes in globalization when human rights are defined ineluctably as global values as well. As Russell West-Pavlov suggests, the space of human rights in the age of globalization is processual difference or becoming as in Deleuze and Guattari's term: "By focusing upon becoming, we focus upon the sensual fabric of existence itself, a fabric which is characterized by . . . difference in time (*devenir*) and space (*multiplicité*)" (241). The denationalization of human rights accounts for this metamorphosis in West-Pavlov's view. As Ferguson and Mansbach explain, space, in this example, national territory, devaluates because of technological advances: "Technological change has played a leading role in devaluing territory" (109).

As Ronaldo Munck argues, human rights and territory decouple in the age of globalization; human rights have validity both in the nation-state and globally. Munck maintains that "human rights are no longer tied exclusively to national sovereignty," and the result is "growing levels of transnational accountability" (78). Human rights are now also subject to global governance, the totality of transnational and global political power and the governing by this power without the existence of a government. Ferguson and Mansbach suggest that principal actors of global governance include institutions, NGOs, TNCs, and MNCs, though in my view people having access to the Internet and global media could also participate in the governance:

> *Multilateral institutions and transnational corporate networks, as well as other public and private institutions that have encouraged and/or been fostered by globalization, are actual or potential sources of global governance.* (78)

Scholars now agree that human rights cannot be merely local. For example, Bauman contends that given the fact of denationalized space, democracy and human rights including freedom can be safeguarded only when these rights are defended globally as well as locally:

> No longer democracy and freedom may be assured in one country or even in a group of countries; their defence in a world saturated with injustice and inhabited by billions of humans denied human dignity would inevitably corrupt the very values they are meant to defend. The future of democracy and freedom may be made secure on a planetary scale— or not at all. ("Liquid Fear" 361)

To Bauman, human rights must be protected globally. To Ferguson and Mansbach, globalization elevates the protection of human rights: "globalization has been accompanied by growing acceptance of individual rights for several decades" (84). "For liberals at least, globalization is believed to promote democracy and wealth, and democracy and wealth promote the 'democratic peace'" (Ferguson and Mansbach 84). To Bauman, Ferguson, Mansbach, and proponents of human rights, globalization promotes human rights, democracy, wealth, and peace by global governance.

Beck and Beck-Gernsheim call human rights' global recognition "cosmopolitanization" (67):

> Cosmopolitanization refers to a state of interdependence between individuals, groups and countries that is not just economic and political but also ethical, transcending national, ethnic, religious and political boundaries and power relations. (67-68)

Cosmopolitans see themselves as members of the human race in addition to being citizens of a nation-state, and Beck, Beck-Gernsheim, Cohen, and Sheringham suggest that cosmopolitanism is a social and communal identity: "Cosmopolitanism is the most universal form of social identity in the sense that it entails the rejection or diminution of all other social categories in favour of the idea of being human" (Cohen and Sheringham 12). Human rights are local and global values because, as the next section will decipher, human rights have a multitude of dimensions.

II. Human Rights' Dimensions

Human rights are both domestic and global values because of the three dimensions I propose in this section.

In the globally extended space, freedom, a cornerstone of all human rights, is an ethical issue as it is a moral, legal, or political polemic in Rainer Frost and Samuel Moyn's explanations, and freedom in all likelihood has incommensurable definitions imparted by nation-states, global politics, and local and international institutions (see fig. 2) (Frost 75-77; Moyn, *The Last* 226-27). I argue that human rights in three dimensions are abstract values, national values, and international and global values (see fig. 2). Human rights, for example, freedom, are abstract concepts and, for this reason, are abstract values. Human rights are national values as the rights are defined by the laws and politics of a nation-state. Moreover, human rights are international and global values in the globally extended space of global civil society and are subject to innumerable and unceasing interpretations by political entities, global politics, global organizations, communities, and individuals. Frost's three perspectives explain human rights as abstract, national, and international and global values (see fig. 2). Moyn's practices of human rights can correspond with all three definitions of mine and all three perspectives of Frost's (see fig. 2).

Human Rights in the Age of Globalization		
Tso's dimensions*	Rainer Frost's three perspectives	Samuel Moyn on the practice of human rights
I. Abstract values	*Ethical*	1. Minimalism in disasters
II. National values	*Political-legal*	2. Utopianism as ideals
III. International and global values	*Political-legal and political-moral*	

Fig. 2. Human Rights in the Age of Globalization.

Frost suggests that human rights are an *"ethical justification,"* and to Frost, Moyn, and Elizabeth Ashford, human rights comprise "autonomy," freedom, "the 'good life,'" and "economic and social rights" (Frost 75-76; Moyn, *Not* 3; Ashford 337-38). Moreover, for Frost, "the *political-legal* aspect or function of human rights" is "in the area of international law" and is not governed merely by the legal system and the politics of a nation-state (76). Frost's third perspective claims that human rights are commensurate with the criteria of these rights among nations: human rights are the *"political-moral* justifications that can be the focus of an international 'overlapping consensus'" (77). Like Frost, Moyn suggests that human rights always carry an ethical and moral aspiration "to transcend politics" either within a nation-state, in transnational and global institutions, or among nations (*The Last* 227). Moreover, Moyn maintains that since the 1970s human rights have evolved from a moral value toward an ever more political one:

> since their explosion in the 1970s human rights have followed a path from morality to politics. . . . Born in the assertion of the 'power of the powerless,' human rights inevitably became bound up with the power of the powerful. (*The Last* 227)

In the practice of human rights, the two ends of the spectrum are minimalism and utopianism as Moyn explicates (see fig. 2):

> In fact, it was due to minimalism and utopianism, indissociably and together, that human rights made their way in the world. . . . Today, these goals— preventing catastrophe through minimalist ethical

63

norms and building utopia through maximalist political vision—are absolutely different. (*The Last* 226)

I will discuss human rights in the matrices of the nation-state and the globally extended space in the next section.

III. Human Rights within the Nation-State and Globally: Not Antagonistic to Nationalism or Isolationism

I maintain that human rights are not antagonistic to nationalism within the national territory, or to isolationism in the globally distended space. Oppositions to human rights arise because human rights flow with fewer impediments than politics and people in the globally extended space. Cristina Lafont alerts people to "the danger of constructing state sovereignty and human rights

64

as antithetical principles" (56). Sharyn Roach Anleu has the same observation, and Roach Anleu's first two "facets or manifestations of human rights discourses" pit human rights against national interests (250). Roach Anleu's four discursive facets of human rights are foreign intervention, dualism between human rights and nationalism, "a strategy or claim" of philanthropic or environmental NGOs, and supporting or indifferent reactions to the third facet (251-53). The purported, not apodictic, rivalry at all times between human rights and the nation-state some people imagine could rest on the fact that values such as human rights flow with much more ease and speed across national borders than politics and people. Both Castells and Bauman write insightfully about this point:

Most certainly, political institutions inherited from two centuries of modern democracy did not follow the economy into global space. The result, as Manuel Castells put it, is a world in which power flows in the uncontrolled and under-institutionalized *global* space, while *politics* stay as *local* as before. (Bauman, "Media" 301)

When human rights claims clash with national interests, Seyla Benhabib argues that a middle point can be attained somewhere between "legal pluralism" recognizing laws other than domestic ones and "national sovereigntism" (38). Like Frost, Benhabib, and Lafont, I argue that human rights are not an anathema to nationalism domestically, or isolationism internationally. In the next section, I will examine three stances of anti-globalization movements on human rights issues in the globally extended space.

IV.   Human Rights and Anti-globalization

Anti-globalization movements and consciousness can remain neutral to human rights, enforce human rights, or infringe human rights. Neomercantilism, a recent form of economic protectionism, is mostly neutral, though it could be insidious, in the issue of human rights beyond national borders. By contrast, the anti-globalization movements launched by NGOs and philanthropic organizations preserve or secure global human rights. Recent anti-globalization movements and consciousness that could imperil human rights of noncitizens include unfair trade policies, unethical entrepreneurialism, drug and human trafficking, terrorism, and dangers of local or global scales. Finally, NGOs with human rights, environmental, and feminist concerns wield more political power by relieving plights and averting dangers locally and globally.

Neomercantilism is a form of economic nationalism. Barry Buzan maintains that advocates of neomercantilism

> make the international economy fit with the patterns of fragmentation in the political system by reducing the scope of the global market. They emphasize the integrity of the national economy and the primacy of state goals (military, welfare, societal). They advocate protection as a way of preserving integrity, but may be attracted to the construction of their own economy dominating at the centre. (qtd. in Ferguson and Mansbach 262)

Ferguson and Mansbach suggest that neomercantilism took form after the global financial crisis:

> Since the onset of the global financial crisis, neomercantilism has experienced a revival, as countries sought ways around trade rules in order to advance their own economic interests. (262)

Anti-globalization movements advancing human rights are often launched by human rights, environmental, or feminist NGOs condemning human rights violations, neoliberal trade agreements, austerity policies, and environmentally damaging practices of industries or corporations. Roach Anleu, for example, defines human rights as the measure or cause of these NGOs:

Human rights discourse is a strategy or claim often made by such NGOs as Amnesty International, Greenpeace, and Human Rights Watch. Such organizations have, among other things, pointed out some of the human rights implications of increasing economic deregulation and liberalization of trade policies via free trade agreements, for example, as leading to increased economic inequalities, especially among the poorest nations and among the poorest members of wealthier nations. (252)

For instance, unemployment and global competition in Bruce O'Neill's research engender the issue of existential boredom for the "homeless and unemployed" in "Romania after the fall of communism" (181). For example, Clifford Bob warns that "the ideology of free trade and the spread of multinational corporations may infringe on labor rights, threaten vulnerable environments, and destroy local control" (144). Some anti-globalists maintain that the rise of the MNCs, TNCs, and outsourcing and subcontracting business strategies may be deleterious to the human rights of non-citizens: "corporate policies and the movement of investment capital to countries with poor environmental and labor standards threaten reductions in living, working, and environmental conditions" (Ferguson and Mansbach 164). Scholars like David Kinley remind business leaders that the TNCs can espouse Corporate Social Responsibility (CSR) to fulfill the promises of human rights in the context of global capitalism (203).

Moreover, the NGOs with human rights, environmental, or feminist agendas gain political power in global as well as local governance as Michael Mascarenhas suggests:

> The relentless expansion of NGOs on the basis of emergency, facilitated by new forms of humanitarian interventions—financial, transnational, and digital, to name only three important features—has resulted in a new and contingent form of sovereignty, where increasingly NGOs are defining and deciding on the state of exception for the world's poor. (313)

Their services at the global level are essential, confronting the dispersion of dangers: our world is "a world of spatially diffuse and omnipresent 'dangers'—global environmental destruction, drugs, terrorism," and epidemics (Ó Tuathail, Herod, and Roberts 12). For example, security is no longer a domestic issue as after the 2001 terrorist attack, the United States tightened border controls and strengthened security from a global standpoint.

Globalization: An Approach
of the Globally Extended Space

Finally, owing to its intersectionality and inclusiveness, globalization has long been a research field of the globally extended space of myriad scholars in social sciences, sciences, the humanities, and other disciplines. Eve Darian-Smith and Philip C. McCarty define globalization as an intersectional approach crossing disciplines and an inclusive methodology in geographical areas in

hearing the voices of scholars "from the global south"
(230):

> a global methodology explicitly widens the lens to
> incorporate a local-global continuum upon which
> one's standpoint can be positioned. Moreover, a
> global methodology takes into account that a person's
> standpoint has numerous intersecting political,
> economic, social, and cultural dimensions and arises
> from intersectional relations of class, race, ethnicity,
> gender, and religion that involve cumulative forms of
> power, oppression, and discrimination. (226)

This stance has long been argued by Stuart Hall to be a fact
in arts and literature. In this book, globalization as
approach is instrumental in the examinations of space,

human rights, and poetry in the global era. Moreover, owing to its interdisciplinarity and inclusiveness, globalization has been one of the topics of general education courses in Taiwan, the United States, and other nations. Students in my university course in globalization studies revel in this field because it is concerned with current events and transformations in the world around them.

Globalization as a methodology combines the merits of both specialization and diversity. First, globalization is an established academic field and approach. Amenable to the scholarship of almost all disciplines, globalization allows scholars to do interdisciplinary research, publish cross-disciplinary articles and books, and teach panoramic courses on catholic topics related to the past and concerned with the status quo historically. Faculty members from myriad departments of a university can adopt globalization as the methodology for general education courses. For example, at my university in 2019, a general education course on globalization examining the Chinese cultural industry in globalization was taught by a professor from the Department of English ("107 xueniandu"). Second, globalization is an apposite methodology for general education courses owing to the diversity of the students coming from a broad array of departments in a university. General education college courses taught in highly specialized methodologies of one or a few disciplines can be irrelevant to the academic or professional goals of a high proportion of students. By contrast, in general education courses on globalization, college students coming from a vast variety of disciplines can develop specialties on one of the diverse aspects of globalization such as its political, environmental, cultural, economic, linguistic, technological, communicative, literary, migratory, criminal, feminist, and social facets. Moreover, general education courses on globalization can be taken with a combination of courses on globalization in departments or schools to confer professional knowledge in the field of globalization. In addition, international students in general education courses are intrigued by the approach of globalization because the canvassed topics are global or transnational, and they also contribute to the transnational and global dialogues in class. "[G]lobalization, transformation from the industrial to the global knowledge economy, and international student mobility are mutually reinforcing one another and changing the higher education landscape worldwide" (Gürüz 15).

Moreover, since globalization is an ongoing process, students of general education courses on globalization explore career goals and opportunities such as new jobs and the globally extended space that globalization is currently actualizing and will provide in the future in the job market, society, and personal life. Globalization is reconfiguring the universities around the world, and an extreme view suggests an interdependence between universities and the global economy:

> Education and the global economy are envisioned as having an interdependent relationship. Competition in the global economy is dependent on the quality of education, whereas the goals of education are dependent on the economy. (Spring 127)

In my view, globalization opens up opportunities for travelers and migrants crossing national borders, people grasping universal human rights, and people with skills for the global capitalist market. Elites, refugees, and migrants move from national territories into the globally extended space for safety, jobs, or better lifestyles. People respecting human rights are accepted by the global civil society, but people who do not conform to global human rights standards, for example, sexists and hate crime offenders, are often rejected by foreign societies or are penalized by the local laws of the host countries. Moreover, a growing number of the elite or people receiving wages lower than those of the host countries will work in the globally extended space in the future. In general education courses on globalization, college students make forays into their career goals and the radical changes in the job market, society, and life in the globally extended space to tackle impending transformations in a world where globalization is a process in progress.

Conclusion

In this chapter, I argue in my theory on space that the extension of space in the ever globalized world enhances freedom or leads to the revamp of the idea of freedom. I explain this theory in four sections of this chapter. In section I, I suggest that human rights are also global values as the space of human rights transmutes and deterritorializes in globalization. In Section II, I argue in my three dimensions of human rights that human rights are abstract values, national values, and international and global values. On account of these three dimensions, freedom as an ethical and a moral, legal, and political value could have conflicting definitions nationally and globally (Frost 75-77; Moyn, *The Last* 226-27). Human rights flow more smoothly than politics and people in the globally extended space. Section III suggests that human rights are not on bad terms with nationalism within national territories, or with isolationism globally. I maintain in Section IV that anti-globalization movements can remain neutral to human rights, safeguard human rights, or infringe human rights. Moreover, globalization is an approach and field of countless scholars and scientists across disciplines and of the globally extended space owing to its intersectionality and inclusivity. Human rights, including freedom, are local values in national territories and global values in the globally extended space, or global civil society.

Part II

The Extension of Space in Poetry

Chapter 4

Taiwanese Poetry on the Globally Extended Space: Freedom, Territoriality, Nostalgia for Space, Solitude, Global Travel, Interconnectedness, and Fear

Introduction

This chapter will exposit the impacts of the globally extended space on freedom, the mind, place, and poetics expressed in modern and contemporary Taiwanese poetry published after the mid-1950s—after the Nationalist government retreated to Taiwan. I will explore mainly the globally extended space in the poetry of two poets— Taiwanese poet Chou-yu Cheng and Taiwanese woman poet Wan-yu Lin. I will also examine the poems on the globally extended space written by Taiwanese women poets Hsiung Hung, Hsia Yu, and Yin Ling. These poets publishing their oeuvres in Taiwan after the midcentury extol global sacrifices for freedom and interpret the territoriality of a nation-state in the globally extended space as sojourning, national security, and diaspora. They affirm the authority of national borders, portray nostalgia for a nation-state's territories, for cultural and linguistic heritages, and for the space of childhood. They reflect on the intensification of loneliness by cyber frauds and the commercialization of human relationships in both virtual and physical space and the alleviation of solitude by global travel. They ponder the dominance of the unconscious in jet lag and the dominancy of the space of childhood in space lag for a globetrotter and attest to global connectivity among strangers. And they chronicle the redefinition of freedom in the globally extended space by global politics and suggest fear to be the primary emotion of people confronting wars and global politics.

Among the five poets, Taiwanese poet Chou-yu Cheng valorizes freedom by lauding global sacrifices for freedom. Chou-yu Cheng identifies three current issues concerned with a nation-state's territoriality in the globally extended space including sojourning, national security, and diaspora and affirms the authority of the borders of nation-states. Moreover, he portrays the nostalgia for the territories of the nation-state and for cultural and linguistic heritages of a person leaving the territories. Wan-yu Lin and Hsia Yu chronicle the power of the Internet, capitalism, and global travel in intensifying global interconnectedness and shaping people's lives today. Wan-yu Lin muses over loneliness intensified by frauds and the commercialization of human relationships in both cyberspace and physical space and the allaying of solitude by global travel. Hsia

Yu's book of poems *First Person* explores global interconnectedness among strangers in a poetics of interrelatedness and openness.

Hsiung Hung elucidates the surfacing of the unconscious for a globetrotter experiencing jet lag and the preeminence of the space of childhood for this traveler in space lag. Moreover, Hsiung Hung interprets the nostalgia for space of childhood. In addition, Yin Ling illuminates the reformulation of freedom in the globally extended space more by global politics than by a nation and expresses the idea that fear is the feeling first and foremost people have confronting wars and global politics in the globally extended space. This last observation is in accordance with Chou-yu Cheng's idea of the second America, the thorny issue of national security for Americans in the globally extended space.

In the ideas of space, the Taiwanese poets discussed in this chapter construe the globally extended space as affective, deterritorializing, related, and interrelated. Moreover, Chou-yu Cheng's and Yin Ling's poetry illustrates my theory on the extension of space and human rights. The globally extended space is affective in Chou-yu Cheng's poetry and deterritorializing in Chou-yu Cheng's, Wan-yu Lin's, Hsia Yu's, and Yin Ling's poems. Wan-yu Lin's and Hsiung Hung's poetry explores relatedness in the social dimension and the affective secondary dimension of space. Wan-yu Lin's and Hsia Yu's poetry probes interrelatedness in my social and international dimension and the virtual secondary dimension of space. Chou-yu Cheng's poems give examples for my theory that the extension of space secures or redefines human freedom. Yin Ling's poetry intimates that with the extension of space human rights including freedom are transformed more by global politics than by nation-states. Chou-yu Cheng's, Hsia Yu's, and Yin Ling's poetry delves into the three dimensions of freedom I propound as an abstract value, a national value, and an international and global value.

Chou-yu Cheng on Freedom, the Significance of the Globally Extended Space, and the Nostalgia for Territories and Heritages

Before embarking on a close reading of Chou-yu Cheng's poems on the globally extended space, a brief critical look at the reception of his poetry and his *ars poetica* will anchor the reading I will offer in a larger context. Based in the United States and Taiwan, Taiwanese poet Wen-tao Cheng, writing under the *nom de plume* Chou-yu Cheng, was born in 1933 in Jinan, a city in Shandong province, China, and migrated to Taiwan with his family in 1949 (Hsu-Hui Ting 45). Chou-yu Cheng earned a B. A. in statistics from the former National Chung Hsing University, now National Taipei University, in 1952, a Master of Fine Arts from the Iowa Writers' Workshop in 1972, and enrolled in the Ph.D. program in Mass Communication at the University of Iowa (Hsu-Hui Ting 46; "Zheng Chouyu nianbiao" 279; "Chubanren" 385-86). Chou-yu Cheng received the Sun Yat-Sen Literature and Arts Award in 1967, the National Award for Arts in 1995, the Global Life Literary Creativity Award of Chou Ta-

Kuan Cultural and Educational Foundation in 2011, and many other prizes from Taiwan, the United States, and elsewhere (Hsu-Hui Ting 47, 59, 67; "Chubanren" 387-88). Chou-yu Cheng went to the United States at the invitation of the University of Iowa's writing program in 1968, had been lecturer teaching Asian Studies at the University of Iowa from 1969 to 1972, and had taught at Yale University from 1973 to 2004, from where he retired in 2004 ("Zheng Chouyu nianbiao" 277-78; Hsu-Hui Ting 48; "Chubanren" 386). He then taught at universities and colleges in the United States, Taiwan, China, and other nations ("Chubanren" 386-87). Chou-yu Cheng married Mai-feng Yu (Mei-fang Yu) in 1962 in Taipei, Taiwan and has three children (Tsun-shing Chen; Hsu-Hui Ting, "Wenxue" 47; "Zheng Chouyu nianbiao" 279). Chou-yu Cheng is currently Professor Emeritus at National Quemoy University in Kinmen County, Taiwan starting from August 2019.[1]

Chou-yu Cheng in the Eyes of Critics and His Ars Poetica

Critical consensus suggests that Chou-yu Cheng writes in a broad array of styles, of which the chief style is a refined and delicate one. Moreover, most critics maintain that while the sense of modernity has informed his poetry and enlivens it with vivid imagery, in his lexicon Chou-yu Cheng interposes words of this time with classical diction. On styles, Chien Chang suggests that Chou-yu Cheng's early poetry is "crystalline, subtle, and flowing," and that the poetry of his middle and late phases is crystalline, subtle, and "obscure" in style ("Zheng" 3).[2] Du Ye suggests that Chou-yu Cheng writes in three styles—"dainty (restrained or feminine), grand (masculine), and grotesque (eccentric)" (55). Both Meng Fan and Tsui-Ying Lee think that in Chou-yu Cheng's poetry the beauty is feminine, in tune with the subtle or dainty style in Chien Chang's and Du Ye's terms, respectively (Meng Fan 209; Tsui-Ying Lee 1). On the language of Chou-yu Cheng, Yang Mu maintains that Chou-yu Cheng "writes in fine Chinese words. . . . And his poetry is absolutely modern" ("Zheng" 11). Likewise, to Wei-jie Zhuang, Chou-yu Cheng's poetry "is pervaded with the intrigue of classical poetry and replete with modern consciousness" (29). In addition, Meng Fan praises the "vivid images, so-called 'painting in poetry'" in Chou-yu Cheng's poetry (210).

In my view, Chou-yu Cheng will be remembered in

literary history as a poet, a literary eminence, writing in an elegant modern language and Western forms on the ocean, love, women, existence, and universal human rights. The roamer as the protagonist or narrator, female characters, the femininity of language, and romances in his poetry captivate many of his readers. Chou-yu Cheng is famed for minting a new language by borrowing phrases, pathos, and settings in classical Chinese literature to render events, objects, and people of the modern world often with acumen. A great number of Chou-yu Cheng's poems are drawn from the poet's own life. The most acute experiences leading to the births of myriad poems are from the poet's childhood during the Second World War and his trips across the globe. In my opinion, Chou-yu Cheng's early poems on the ocean and love and his most recent poems on geopolitics and life, for example, the poem "Three United States of America," are his finest works. On migration, wars, and love, the early poems such as the poem "Mistake" published in the decades after the Second World War enchant both the roving soul of the people migrating from China and the postcolonial mind of the Taiwanese suppressed by and suffering under the Japanese empire. More poems in the late phase on universal topics including freedom, humaneness, and human existence capture the imagination of a globalized Taiwan seeking international recognition and respect. Chou-yu Cheng's poems "The Eternity of Václavské Square" and "You Did Not Return from the Trip" examined in this chapter are two poems on these topics.

Chou-yu Cheng's own *ars poetica* suggests that human nature and forms are two of his primary concerns in poetry. For example, to Chou-yu Cheng, "the depth of poetry is human nature" (qtd. in Mong Li 14). Moreover, for Chou-yu Cheng, content has priority over form: the poet "creates different forms for the contents" (Broadcasting Corporation of China). For this reason, to Chou-yu Cheng, experimenting with form is the task for modern poets: "owing to disparate expressions of emotions, modern poets often must devise new forms for the contents" (Chou-yu Cheng, "Yong" 17).

Chou-yu Cheng on Freedom, Territoriality,

and the Nostalgia for Territories and Heritages

In this section, I will examine five poems on the globally extended space in globalization written by Chou-yu Cheng including "The Eternity of Václavské Square," "You Did Not Return from the Trip," "Three United States of America," "Border Inn," and "Celeste Sky." Chou-yu Cheng's poems "The Eternity of Václavské Square" and "You Did Not Return from the Trip" supply examples to my theory that the extension of space ensures or redefines freedom in proportion to the degree of extension. His poem "Three United States of America" suggests that in globalization, the concept of the nation-state's territory is being reconfigured by issues including sojourning, national security, and diaspora in physical, virtual, and imagined space in both newly created transnational and global space and space within the nation-state. Chou-yu Cheng's poem "Border Inn" interprets nostalgia as pensiveness for the territory of the nation-state a person leaves and suggests that the borders of the nation-state still have legal power and stature. Another poem "Celeste Sky" explains nostalgia as the wistfulness a person has for cultural or linguistic heritages.

Chou-yu Cheng's poem "The Eternity of Václavské Square" affirms martyrs' sacrifices for freedom during the Prague Spring at Václavské Square, or Wenceslas Square, in the former Czech and Slovak Federative Republic, now the Czech Republic, in 1968; during the Huanghuagang Uprising in Guangzhou, China in 1911; and during the Tiananmen Square Tragedy at Tiananmen Square, China in 1989 (Lin, Lin, Pang, and Liu 36). The throes of the Chinese people's failed striving for freedom in 1989 moved Chou-yu Cheng to write the poem "The Eternity of Václavské Square." Chou-yu Cheng experiences the afflatus of the poem "The Eternity of Václavské Square" during a trip to Poland and the former Czech and Slovak Federative Republic, now the Czech Republic, in 1990 ("Caixiang" 12). On June 4, 1990, Chou-yu Cheng saw Polish students at the University of Warsaw mourn the Tiananmen Square Tragedy at the incident's first anniversary when he visited the university in Warsaw, Poland ("Caixiang" 12; Hsu-Hui Ting 55). On June 5, 1990, while Chou-yu Cheng witnessed the election of the president in the former Czech and Slovak Federative Republic, "June 4 was still on his mind," and he had "the inspiration of a poem" ("Caixiang" 12).

Chou-yu Cheng aimed to "become a poet of humanitarianism" after receiving praises from his teacher about the spirit of humanitarianism in his first poem on Chinese miners (Broadcasting Corporation of China). Chinfeng Tseng and many scholars also notice the spirit of humanitarianism in his poetry (Tseng 24). Bai Ling explains this spirit of humanitarianism as the poet's civil consciousness: Chou-yu Cheng is "a chivalric person while facing society" ("The Traveller" 148). Like Tseng, Bai Ling, and many other critics, Mei-Fang Chang suggests that Chou-yu Cheng's poetry "espouses benevolence" (77).

Chou-yu Cheng selects Wenceslas Square as the setting for his poem "The Eternity of Václavské Square," a eulogy on martyrs of freedom ("Caixiang" 14). A note on the poem explains that many revolts took place at Wenceslas Square including the May uprising of people in 1945 and Prague Spring in 1968 (*Jimo* 71). This note of Chou-yu Cheng suggests that people in Prague mourned the martyrs of these two and other uprisings.

The opening of the poem "The Eternity of Václavské Square" comments on the history of the square as an ancient horse market and on the self's expansion in the square's open space. The narrator from the East feels pious yet strange among the statues of saints on the square. The sudden and heavy rain falling on the square like herds of horses reminds the narrator of the intrusion of Warsaw

Pact troops into the square ("Czech"; Golan 236). Ironically, the Chinese phrase "in a short while" literally means "Soviet in a while." Thunder at the square is reminiscent of the "war drums" in 1968. Chou-yu Cheng explains in an essay that the heavy rain's scale "reproduces the war," and like the rain in the poem "The Eternity of Václavské Square," in 1989, "a heavy rain pelted down suddenly and pitifully washed away the blood stains" in the capital of China ("Caixiang" 14).

After the rain ceases, without delay the inhabitants of Prague prayed and lighted candles for Czech war martyrs.

Entering the Horse Gate   I faintly heard the ancient horse market's

neighs. Stopping   my sleeves gathering wind

my torso huger with each breath

an easterner among the statues of Western saints, I

felt strange and pious.

In a short while   a torrential rain suddenly fell   like

one troop after another troop of winning steeds galloping around the

square until . . .

the rain ceased. Thunder was as distant as the war drums

beyond the mountain. Inhabitants of the city scurried out from their

eaves to light fires and pray in indistinct rumbles of drums.

. . . .

Ah, the commemoration of the nation's martyrs

cannot stop one single day (*Jimo* 68-69)

The square is below "the statues of saints" and among "the
National Museum, the library," and the former "Federal
Parliament" of the former Czech and Slovak Federative
Republic as the poem "The Eternity of Václavské Square"
and a note following the poem explain (*Jimo* 69, 71;

Velinger). The flowers and candles are in front of photos of young Czechs, the poem next recounts (*Jimo* 69). The easterner in the poem may also be a Christian if the narrator is modeled after the poet Chou-yu Cheng. Chou-yu Cheng was baptized in 1948 "at an Anglican church in the school" in China and has been a Christian since because Chou-yu Cheng said that he "had committed to be one" (Tsun-shing Chen).

Next, the narrator concludes that in these uprisings, the significance of freedom is the martyrs' sacrifices:

The square (Rain once washed away the blood stains)

The citizens enkindled fires (Candles started to burn)

(Ah, candles   to leave their bodies   gained freedom with burning?)

The citizens prayed   Flowers were in full bloom

(Ah, flowers   to leave the form   gained freedom by withering?)

And martyrs   while spring was there   chose to die as soldiers

Deities   were thus canonized   Then   the purport of freedom,

is what if not sacrifice? (*Jimo* 69-70)

The martyrs are deified by sacrificing their lives fighting for freedom in the country, the narrator suggests. Following this, the inhabitants of Prague sing when the winds drop (*Jimo* 70). The narrator suggests that "the heat of spring" is from "the warmth concealed for a long time in the heart of every seed" (*Jimo* 70). In the closing of "The Eternity of Václavské Square," the narrator interrelates the many uprisings for freedom in the former Czech and Slovak Federative Republic and two uprisings in China, the 1911 Huanghuagang Uprising leading to the collapse of the Qing empire, and the 1989 Tiananmen Square Tragedy. Next, "The Eternity of Václavské Square" contrasts the two places, Huanghuagang and Tiananmen Square. The deaths of the Chinese martyrs during the Huanghuagang Uprising encouraged the people about the revolution and contributed to the success of the next uprising that ended the Qing Dynasty (Lin, Lin, Pang, and Liu 37). People have long forgotten the martyrs of the Huanghuagang Uprising, but the Chinese still packed Tiananmen Square in 1989 where the mourners were dispersed by troops. The narrator of "The Eternity of Václavské Square" relates:

> At this moment   that foreigner
>
> stood silently   shirtsleeves drooping like a candle in trance
>
> And fire   burned inwards . . .

Yet, in scorching pain the easterner, recalling

the Huanghuagang few visited and

the frequented bleak Tiananmen Square, and

thinking about the inhabitants of Beijing weeping secretly

even while visiting tombs, also burned inwards like candles . . .

Ah, would the five internal organs

digest the tears hot as fire throughout this life? (*Jimo* 70)

The narrator cannot but weep for the Chinese martyrs too. "The Eternity of Václavské Square" ends with the narrator's mourning for the martyrs of freedom. The tears of the narrator are likened to the flows of the candles' wax. The narrator sheds tears at the closing of the poem for the martyrs and for freedom not yet attained in the world.

"The Eternity of Václavské Square" portrays people's mourning in Beijing because the first event of the 1989

Tiananmen Square Tragedy was the mourning of Hu Yaobang, a former chairman of the Chinese Communist Party, by students at Tiananmen Square on April 15, 1989 the day Hu died (Minzhu 5-6; "Hua"). Hu was tolerant toward student demonstrations and "Western political and cultural influences" (Minzhu 5-6). Hu is a more popular leader than Deng Xiaoping to the students (Minzhu 6). Mourning Hu was part of the student protests at Tiananmen Square in April 1989 (Feng 85).

Chou-yu Cheng maintains that martyrdom and patriotism depicted in "The Eternity of Václavské Square" are central to his poetics. Chou-yu Cheng said that "the spirit of a knight" "lifted to the height of a revolution becomes the spirit of martyrs and assassins. This is also a mainstay of my poetry" (qtd. in Liao 67). Hsiao Hsiao and

Wen-Ling Luo agree that the image Chou-yu Cheng builds in his poetry is that of "a benevolent knight" or a patriot ready to sacrifice for the country (2). Hsiao Hsiao and Luo define "a benevolent knight" as a person who chooses the nation-state instead of the family when there is only one choice (2).

The note following Chou-yu Cheng's poem "You Did Not Return from the Trip" published in 1992 suggests that Polish musician and pianist Fryderyk Chopin did not return to Poland, his homeland, "because of freedom" (Hsu-Hui Ting 57; *Jimo* 78). Freedom is one of the uppermost values to Chou-yu Cheng as to the Polish musician. Chou-yu Cheng writes in his note to "You Did Not Return from the Trip" that he experienced "the means of the totalitarian system" when he travelled in 1990 from

Poland to "the former Czech and Slovak Federative Republic, to Austria, and next to Hungary" by the Chopin Express (*Jimo* 78); he was closely examined by border police and soldiers on this train journey, "awakened many times by armed inspectors" as the poem's note and the poem portray (*Jimo* 77-78).

Chopin left for Vienna in 1830, travelled to Munich in 1831, and next went to Württenmerg that year ("Chronology" ix; Atwood 47). Chopin left Stuttgart, Württenmerg for Paris in 1831 when he heard the news that Warsaw was under the Russian Empire's military control (Atwood 53-54). Owing to his financial situation in Paris, Chopin once thought about returning to Warsaw, Poland (Karasowski 260). Chopin decided not to return to Poland and instead earned additional income by giving piano lessons to the family of Prince Valentine Radziwill in Paris (Karasowski 260). Chopin obtained a residence permit in Paris, did not return to Poland, and died in Paris in 1849 (Atwood 55, 192).

Chou-yu Cheng also spent years of exile in the United States after his ROC passport was revoked because from 1970 to 1971 he had twice been the chair of the Diaoyu Islands activist movement at the University of Iowa ("Zheng Chouyu nianbiao" 278; *Taiwan History*). In 1979 Chou-yu Cheng was allowed to return to Taiwan to attend his father's funeral (Chou-yu Cheng, *Zheng Chouyu shiji I* 331).

The opening of the poem "You Did Not Return from the Trip" suggests that Chopin did not return to Warsaw, Poland after a trip to Vienna: "You did not return from your

travel" (*Jimo* 76). "You Did Not Return from the Trip"
recounts that trains left nightly from Warsaw. Just as the
Viennese adore Mozart, the Poles without freedom love
Chopin the expatriate, the poem next suggests. The train
passengers

> wondered   how could your old country losing its freedom in 1849
>
> take the news of your death.
>
> You buried yourself with the soil of your old country you brought
>
> at a place your love chose to dwell
>
> You were therefore buried in the hearts of people who love you
>
> Human beings love you and love freedom
>
> For this reason everyone's heart is your cenotaph (*Jimo* 77)

The poem's ending reminds the reader of Chopin's country
of origin with the story about the soil Chopin received

before he departed for Vienna. Right before Chopin left Poland in 1830, he received a goblet of the soil of Poland as a present at a banquet held for him in Poland (Karasowski 156-57).

Moreover, on territoriality in the globally extended space, Chou-yu Cheng's poem "Three United States of America" interprets the territoriality of the United States as three Americas—the space of sojourning, American national security, and diaspora in the globally extended space. Among these three renderings of the territoriality of the United States, the second America represents the issue of American national security. The narrator's family currently lives in "the third America" as members of a diaspora in the United States (*Jimo* 188):

We live in the third America   in the same

continent   The contents of our lives are much more old-fashioned

We spend half of our time missing the place afar

and spend another half of the time incessantly reviewing

the essence of the culture of hair and skin

in the cuisine   at times of the frequent warm gatherings with

relatives and friends

What we miss and review is this verity (Jimo 188)

By contrast, the first America is the land of sojourning where foreigners travel, work, or study:

Yet often we discuss

the first America

where we competed, travelled, smiled, and used our brains to

undertake activities of laws

We sent our children there and took them back,

earned money carefully   and paid it meticulously

This first America is bright   under one

sun   where we entered and left but fantasized it to be the flickering

and strepitous

shadows of dreams (*Jimo* 188-89)

Furthermore, the second America is the abstract concept of the United States as a nation-state on the map and a land where Americans live with other fellow citizens. "Three United States of America" portrays national security as a central concern of American citizens very close to their daily lives. "Three United States of America" next relates that the national security of the United States and Americans' safety are under threats including climate change and extraterrestrial wars. The poem compares the threatened national security of the United States to its national flag fluttering in freezing gusts. Earthquakes are major natural disasters in the United States. The topic of national security in globalization "Three United States of America" explores is still a current issue decades after the poem was composed. Wars and threats in outer space made U.S. President Donald Trump order in 2018 a "Memorandum on Establishment of the United States Space Force" to "establish a United States Space Force as a sixth branch of the United States Armed Forces within the Department of the Air Force" (1). Potential warfare in outer space is a national security crisis for Americans then and today:

And there is the second America overlapping and

close-by. It is the proximity of the air that looms up

The color of the territory is peculiar   at the same

temperature   in the safety of the cycles of winters and summers

yet hoists a flag of nippy winds

and endures the earthquakes of fires

(Will it rain tomorrow? Will there be wars in outer space?)

We will still live in the third America

missing   reviewing   discussing

pretending nothing is closing in toward us (*Jimo* 189-90)

The characters in "Three United States of America" live and will live in the third America, a diaspora in the United States, missing loved ones far away in the source country they emigrate from and remembering its culture.

Fears about natural disasters, wars in outer space, and other menaces to national security can only be suppressed in pretense, "Three United States of America" suggests.

Feargal Cochrane's comment on the post-9/11 national security of the United States explains to a certain extent the proximity of the threats:

> The umbilical cord between the two points of security and migration was frequently a short one, not least in the US, where almost immediately after the 9/11 attacks, the Immigration and Naturalization Service (INS) was moved within the new Department of Homeland Security. Thus, even in terms of its governance and administration, the US was making a statement that the security of the homeland was dependent upon keeping a closer record of those who were either physically or politically beyond it. (5)

However, the narrator of "Three United States of America," a member of a diaspora, may not represent all members of a diaspora or an ethnic group. Both Cochrane and Ien Ang oppose the idea of "groupism" or group stereotypes in judging diasporic members and migrants in globalization in the "new transnational spaces for contemporary understandings of security at both national and international levels" created by globalization (Ang 27; Cochrane 152). Ang defines groupism as "the tendency to take discrete, sharply differentiated, internally homogenous and externally bounded groups as basic constituents of social life" (5). Cochrane recommends "greater knowledge of the diversity and complexity of migrant communities on the part of policy-makers" (168). "Instead a more processual and flexible understanding is proposed [by Ang] where the relationship between 'ethnic' and 'national' identity is one of constant evolution and mutual entanglement" (Ang 27).

National security or the second America in "Three United States of America" resonates with the theme of war in Chou-yu Cheng's virtuoso early poem "Mistake." Published in 1954, "Mistake" brings the memories of wars and migration in China to life for Chou-yu Cheng and for countless readers with the romantic "waiting of a woman for her husband at war or son" (Hsu-Hui Ting 46; *Wandering*). Chou-yu Cheng maintains that a number of his poems are wrought from the suffering and wars in China in his "unconscious" because "he grew up during the Sino-Japanese war as a child" (qtd. in Liao 67). The woman in "Mistake," as Chou-yu Cheng suggests, is the persona for the young boy Chou-yu Cheng and his mother (*Cuowu*). The mother and son missed the father serving in the Chinese military during the Sino-Japanese war while they moved across China for safety (*Cuowu*).

In addition to the issues of freedom and travel in the globally extended space explored in "The Eternity of Václavské Square," "You Did Not Return from the Trip," and "Three United States of America," the entrenched authority of the borders of the nation-state in the globally extended space is most emphatically expressed in Chou-yu Cheng's early poem "Border Inn" published in 1965 (*Cheng Chou-yu shi* 246). The globally extended space is the space conjoining various nations' territories in globalization and includes both the new virtual and transnational space begotten in globalization and national territories. "Border Inn" interprets the nostalgia for the territory of a nation-state as affection arising after deterritorialization or leaving the land of a nation-state. "Border Inn" repudiates, thus, the breaking down of the borders of the embattled nation-states in the globally extended space in globalization, suggesting instead that the nation-state's territory is impervious to the redefinitions of the land conceptually and jurisdictionally by irregular migrants, sojourners without legal documents, and traffickers. In autumn the narrator of "Border Inn" is at a place near the borders between two nation-states:

> The territories in autumn divided their borders under one setting sun
>
> At the place the soil abutted, some yellow chrysanthemums stood silently
>
> And travelling from afar, he was sober and was drinking
>
> Out of the window was a foreign country (*Cheng Chou-yu shi* 245)

The narrator imagines that by crossing the border the

narrator could experience nostalgia for the nation the narrator is now in. The "beautiful" concept of nostalgia to the narrator is so tangible as it could be realized within a short distance (*Cheng Chou-yu shi* 245). Zhong-Yi Chen suggests that the next line on the crossing over has the strongest tension in this poem (26):

How much did I desire to cross over. One step, and nostalgia was achieved

That beautiful nostalgia, tangible by the reach of my hand

(*Cheng Chou-yu shi* 245)

The sober narrator next wishes to cross the border when drunk and is even willing to pay taxes in the foreign country. In the end of the poem, the narrator thinks about singing because by singing the narrator is better than the chrysanthemums doing nothing by the borders:

Or, got drunk

(He was an enthusiastic taxpayer)

Or, sang

In this way he did not just stand like that chrysanthemum

only standing by the borders

(*Cheng Chou-yu shi* 245-46)

The chrysanthemum and the narrator in "Border Inn" do not cross over to another nation in the closing of the poem. The narrator interprets nostalgia as leaving the territory of the nation-state and would like to feel nostalgic about the country on this side of the border. But a nation's border is a strict legal and political line, and ultimately the narrator does not cross over to another nation-state's territory. The narrator suggests that a person can at least sing about the desire to feel nostalgic about the space a person leaves such as a nation's territory.

Unlike the poem "Border Inn," Chou-yu Cheng's poem "Celeste Sky" portrays the nostalgia for one's own culture and language in a foreign country. Additionally, "Celeste Sky" focuses on the spatial distance in aesthetics the color celeste connotes. The color celeste evokes the narrator's nostalgia for Chinese cultural and linguistic heritages. The poem "Celeste Sky" renders physical space into cultural and affective space; the latter is the secondary dimension of my social dimension of space. The narrator under the celeste sky of Quebec, Canada recalls the color celeste in Chinese culture and language:

Parted only by a windowpane—

the celeste sky, in fact, did not announce anything

Celeste for long is a formidable color to define

is the color of eyebrows—the freshly drawn shade

is the pigment of a hairstyle of children's unloosed hair

is the tint of blood . . . coursing in blood vessels

Who said that celeste sky like this

was Canada's high-pressure air masses in actuality

Was the voice, was it not a bit like

Quebec's quaint French accent

In verity, celeste is a color of distance

the chromism of grass—on the other shore

the hue of mountain ranges—beyond a pass

A dialect's short distance—the hearer, for this, felt some

nostalgia

in Nova Scotia, Canada (*Yanrenxing* 53-54)

The poem "Celeste Sky" explores "all the 'nostalgia' about 'celeste' in history," suggests Chou-yu Cheng ("Se" 26-27). The history of the color celeste came to his mind right after a car trip in Quebec, Canada ("Se" 26-27). Chou-yu Cheng drove a car to a high place in Quebec where the sky seemed to interblend with the "plain" and St. Lawrence Seaway in "a 'celeste' realm like in fantasy" ("Se" 26). When he turned on the radio, the voice in French "seemed to say that the high pressure let us experience a vaster Quebec," Chou-yu Cheng recalls about the car trip ("Se" 26). When he reached Nova Scotia in northeast Canada, a place he "visited annually," Chou-yu Cheng composed this poem "Celeste Sky" ("Se" 27; *Zheng Chouyu is at*). In addition, as the history of the color celeste in this poem exemplifies, to Chou-yu Cheng the ideas in poetry are founded on culture. Chou-yu Cheng expounds this foundation of culture in a 2017 speech: "If ideas are not constructed on the foundations of culture, the ideas you get are probably ephemeral—like a night-blooming cereus" ("Cong").

Moreover, Chou-yu Cheng maintains that the color celeste intimates at once beauty and spatial distance and is the aesthetic color for green or blue. "Celeste is an abstract color," Chou-yu Cheng argues ("Yong" 30). "Mountain ranges outside a pass (distance) are called 'celeste mountain ranges.' Only a place with white clouds in the sky is called a celeste mountain. Distance is one of the elements that produce beauty," comments Chou-yu Cheng on the color celeste in the poem "Celeste Sky" ("Se" 27).

To sum up, Chou-yu Cheng's two poems on freedom

and space examined, "The Eternity of Václavské Square" and "You Did Not Return from the Trip," support my theory that in the age of globalization, the extension of space to a certain extent safeguards or redefines freedom in proportion to the degree of extension. In their eulogies for the martyrs of freedom, Chou-yu Cheng and the narrator of "The Eternity of Václavské Square" bring the status of the value of freedom to a new height. Moreover, both Chopin and Chou-yu Cheng travelled across the globe to achieve world fame and to secure freedom. In addition, Chou-yu Cheng maintains that owing to the nature of poetry as a genre, traveling globally in the globally extended space is indispensable for poets. Answering my question about "the relationship between writing literature and a life in various countries and places, and that between the writing of literature and the converging of space among places" in 2017 during his speech, Chou-yu Cheng maintains that "going to various countries and places is of vital importance" because of the genre of poetry ("Cong"). "People writing poetry must travel around," he accentuates ("Cong").

In two other poems "Border Inn" and "Celeste Sky," Chou-yu Cheng defines nostalgia as pathos for the territory a person leaves or for cultural and linguistic heritages, respectively. Chou-yu Cheng advocates for the inviolable borders of the nation-state in his poem "Border Inn." Another poem "Three United States of America" suggests, however, that the territory of the nation-state is being redefined by issues including sojourning, national security, and diaspora in the new globally extended physical space, virtual space, and space in imagination. The globally extended space in globalization is a gripping topic for Wan-yu Lin as it is for Chou-yu Cheng. I will examine Wan-yu Lin's poems on the globally extended space in the next section.

Wan-yu Lin on Solitude, Global Travel, and the Power of Love in the Globally Extended Space

Taiwanese woman poet Wan-yu Lin is the pen name of Chia-yu Lin born in 1977 in Taichung City.[3] After two years in the School of Nutrition and Health Sciences at Taipei Medical University, Wan-yu Lin enrolled in the Department of Theatre Arts at Taipei National University of the Arts, majoring in playwriting, and later received a B. A. Wan-yu Lin's books of poetry include *Things That*

Just Transpired (2007, new edition 2018); *Possible Nectar* (2011), winner of the 11th annual Taipei Literature Award's poetry project; *Those Lightning Bolts Point toward You* (2014), winner of the 2014 poetry prize from *The Best Taiwanese Poetry, 2014*; and *Twenty-four Arithmetic Operations of Love* (2017). Wan-yu Lin told the author in 2019 that to her, her first book of poetry is *Things That Just Transpired*, not her chapbook *Practices of Love* (2001). *Things That Just Transpired* "is the first book of poems" for Wan-yu Lin ("Shi de mohu" 81). Wan-yu Lin won Lin Rong San Literary Prize's third prize for poetry in 2005, the China Times Literary Prize, and other awards. Poetry aside, Wan-yu Lin started writing lyrics for singers including Christine Fan in 2015.

Wan-yu Lin's poetry on globalization and space

chronicles the power of the Internet and global travel in intensifying global interconnectedness and structuring modern people's lives. On globalization and both virtual and physical space, Wan-yu Lin's poetry suggests that the loneliness of modern people is intensified by cyber frauds and the commercialization of human relationships in both virtual and physical space. Moreover, on globalization and physical space, Wan-yu Lin's poetry suggests that the realization of the global village in physical space is one of the dreams of forlorn modern people. Global travel alleviates to a certain degree the problem of modern solitude as modern people take global journeys to reunite with their loved ones across national borders, Wan-yu Lin's poetry suggests.

Wan-yu Lin in Critics' Eyes and Her Ars Poetica

Before moving to a close scrutiny of Wan-yu Lin's poems on the extension of space, in this section I will devote a few words to the critical reception of her poetry and her *ars poetica* as a broader context for the discussion of her poems. A prolific poet who is now a professional writer, Wan-yu Lin has published love poems on omnifarious romances and poems on children, her mother, family members, and towns and cities in Taiwan including but not limited to Guandu, Taichung, and Taipei. Within her oeuvres of refined poetry, Wan-yu Lin is at her best in lyric poems with astute musings on love and on life in our time of globalization and the information age, for example, her poem "Solitude is Real." Wan-yu Lin writes some of the best profound poems on life of this time. The dynamic twenty-first century witnesses revolutions in thoughts and technologies such as the growing importance of social media and Facebook in people's lives and the shifts of power in nation-states and governments in geopolitics to make people experience the clashes among forms of states such as those among democracies, communism, and theocracies, and among the industrialized countries and the source countries of refugees and migrants. A large number of her other poems are soothing as well as bold and frank. The majority of Wan-yu Lin's poems do not state the ideas or the emotions directly or explicitly.

As Wan-yu Lin suggests, most of her poems have fabricated plots, imagined characters, and fictitious situations and are not confessional: "Ideas and imagination weave the fictive plots and stories" of most of her poems

(*Ai* 205). For this reason, poems without references to real people and locales are more luminous than other poems. Wan-yu Lin's poetry is in the rank of contemporary lyric poetry of the self and is moving sometimes even without fancy diction. A contemporary poet writing in this vein in English is the American poet Louise Glück. In Taiwanese poetry, some of Wan-yu Lin's lyric poems resonate with the works of Hsia Yu in astuteness and in feminism and femininity that underlie their poetic agendas. In all, Wan-yu Lin's poetry explores women's stakes, their affections, and their worlds primarily in this millennium.

Many critics note the feelings, the ideas, the light tone, the simple language, the colloquialism, and the transformation of the quotidian into the poetic in Wan-yu Lin's poetry. Ya Hsien comments that Wan-yu Lin "often propounds a profound and elaborate state of feelings in an undramatic language" (15). The comment on Wan-yu Lin's poetry in *Three Hundred New Poems*, an anthology of modern poetry in Chinese, also suggests that her poetry "on a vast array of subject matters written in a succinct, refined, simple, and accessible language can be laden with innermost feelings and insights" ("Pingjian" 885). Likewise, Shing-jie Ling takes the view that the best part of Wan-yu Lin's poetry is "the intensity of feelings" (232). Wan-yu Lin also illuminates the vital importance of the idea in her poetry in her poem "The Fall":

Poetry is like this

always like this: deep and veiled,

undisturbed. (*Ganggang*, 2018 174)

Inmost feelings and discerning astuteness in thoughts are paired with a simple language and a blithe tone in Wan-yu Lin's poetry. Cong-Xiu Zeng maintains that Wan-yu Lin "often can expatiate upon acute feelings in a simple language and images" (130). To Chung-Cheng Yen, her poetry is written in "a light tone. The inner thoughts are heavy and settled though the narrative style is sprightly . . . with a massive use of colloquialism" (126). On Wan-yu Lin's earliest poetry, Chih-cheng Lo maintains that "she creates dramatic (especially comedic) parodies in nimble syntax and witty structures. Moreover, she always touches our hearts or deploys surprises in time before a poem ends" (1). Ya Hsien, Shing-jie Ling, and Shen Mian maintain that she transforms the spoken Chinese of daily life into the poetic (Ya Hsien 8; Ling 232; Shen Mian 21). For example,

Ya Hsien suggests that Wan-yu Lin "turns spoken Chinese into poetry" (8). Likewise, to Shing-jie Ling, Wan-yu Lin "turns the language of the everyday into a literary language" (232). On Wan-yu Lin's book of poems *Those Lightning Bolts Point toward You*, Shen Mian maintains that Wan-yu Lin "mixes the quotidian and the poetic. In other words, hers is an aesthetic of the poetics of life" (22).

Wan-yu Lin agrees with her critics on the weight of ideas in her poetry and with my opinion that her poetry is poetry of the self on life. Wan-yu Lin maintains that "innovativeness, subversion, or deepening" are three of the traits enhancing "the quality of poetry" ("Shi de mohu" 42). The profundity of ideas is coupled with simplicity of language in her poetry as Wan-yu Lin explains: "I definitely do not advance plainness [of "words"]. I just expect the poetic language to let people just perceive the 'idea,'" obviating verbiage on the ineffable (*Naxie* 217). "The 'idea' could perhaps be explained as originality and idea," Wan-yu Lin adds (*Naxie* 217). When she composes poetry, Wan-yu Lin "writes down the ideas triggered [by 'events and objects'] and renders them into poetry" (*Ganggang*, 2007 212). On the self in poetry, Wan-yu Lin declares: "writing is a way to express myself" (qtd. in Emily Chung 183). Her poetry is extremely close to life in subject matter just as Wan-yu Lin commented. When she was a college student at Taipei National University of the Arts, Wan-yu Lin was surrounded by art works and performances, and she developed the idea of the close relationship between art and world: "I feel that writing is life. I do not think that art is a thing that cannot be attained.

I feel that art is related to the world before our eyes" ("Shi de qinggan").

In addition to life, love and people are indispensable elements of her poetry, Wan-yu Lin maintains ("Shi han"). In a 2016 speech on poetry, songs, and the world, Wan-yu Lin defines her *ars poetica* or "the heart of poetry" in three parts including life, love, and accessibility: "The poetry I would like to write is closer to life and to love and can be felt by everyone" ("Shi han"). Moreover, in Wan-yu Lin's view, "the energy of paramount importance in poetry derives from people" (*Naxie* 218). In the next section, I will examine Wan-yu Lin's poems on love and life in the globally extended space in globalization and on global interconnectedness.

Solitude, Global Travel, and Love in the

Globally Extended Space in Globalization

On love in the age of globalization, Wan-yu Lin's poem "Solitude is Real" disparages frauds in interconnected global cyberspace and commerce in physical space for invading and overswarming the space of human relationships. "Solitude is Real" suggests that spam mail and fraudulent correspondence in cyberspace and marketing activities in physical space aggravate the modern crisis of solitude. The narrator in "Solitude is Real" contrasts the veridical loneliness and its worsening by scams in cyberspace and physical space in life, beginning with an emphasis on the frequency of frauds as daily routines:

Every day

such a profuse number of people e-mail me—

junk mail and fraudulent correspondence.

On the streets

such a profuse number of people offer me small presents—

advertising flyers and facial tissue.

Facebook periodically sends me notifications:

"Someone mentioned you on Facebook."

"Someone tagged you in a post."—

disinformation from social shopping communities.

Deceptive

All deceptive—

but solitude is real. (Wan-yu Lin, *Ai* 72-73)

The narrator is almost overwhelmed by fake e-mail messages, advertising leaflets, packets of samples, and commercialized Facebook notifications. Under siege by fake correspondence and contacts in both virtual space and physical space, the narrator's loneliness is more intense.

The Information Revolution in the age of globalization interrelates people globally on the Internet just a few clicks away in *"the culture of real virtuality"* in Castells's term (*End* 386). Castells defines "real virtuality" as

> a system in which reality itself (that is, people's material/symbolic existence) is fully immersed in a virtual image setting, in the world of make believe, in which symbols are not just metaphors, but comprise the actual experience. (*End* 386)

People could accept virtual experience in "real virtuality" as real, as Castells suggests (*End* 386). Moreover, Castells explains his theory on the Internet and capitalist society by stating: the "information technology revolution was instrumental in allowing the implementation of a fundamental process of restructuring of the capitalist system from the 1980s onwards" (*Rise* 13). Castells suggests that "the global economy is now a network of interconnected segments of economies, which play, together, a decisive role in the economy of each country—and of many people" (*Rise* 147).

Wan-yu Lin in her poetry criticizes the consequences of the virtual world's participation in modern life because after the Information Revolution, frauds exploit the Internet networks interrelating people to intrude upon private space and consume time traditionally reserved for human relationships. As Wan-yu Lin's poetry suggests, if people receive a large quantity of unwanted and fake correspondence and frauds, in their disappointment and fury they feel more isolated than connected. "Solitude is Real" recounts that the prodigious correspondence a person receives in cyberspace is sent from nonhumans or is fake. "Junk mail" generated by machines or computer viruses and advertisements from the "social shopping communities" on Facebook, for instance, are not correspondence from friends, relatives, and loved ones (Wan-yu Lin, *Ai* 72-73). "Solitude is Real" points out that the flood of e-mail frauds and Facebook advertising messages pretend to be correspondence seeking to build human relationships. In the physical space within the nation-state, commercial activities transpire more frequently than romance in life, "Solitude is Real" relates. For example, walking on the street, the narrator of "Solitude is Real" receives commercial fliers and packets of tissues as gifts (Wan-yu Lin, *Ai* 72).

In Taiwan, the solitude of celibacy is true because today a higher percentage of Taiwanese are single than nearly two decades ago. In Taiwan, in contrast with the percentage of the married plummeting between 1989 and 2018, the percentage of single people rose between 1989 and 2018 (Department of Household Registration Affairs). For example, the percentage of single people aged 15 and older including the unmarried, divorced, and widowed in Taiwan was 40.73% in 1989 and 49.55% in 2018 (Department of Household Registration Affairs). By contrast, 50.45% of the people aged 15 and older in Taiwan were married in 2018, falling from 59.27% in 1989 (Department of Household Registration Affairs). Another poem "The Fifth Planet of the Little Prince" interprets global travel that contributes to the interconnectedness of people on earth. People take global travels to reunite with loved ones, "The Fifth Planet of the Little Prince" suggests. Global travel by air boosts tourism more in journeys over a vast expanse than in short-distance trips, John Bowen maintains (189). Over 40 percent of tourists travel by air in this millennium (Bowen 189).

"The Fifth Planet of the Little Prince" recounts that the physical global village, embodied by "the smallest of all planets," the fifth planet, is the dream of solitary people (*Naxie* 130):

On the minute and minute

the fifth planet of the little prince, which a person

could go around in five steps,

walking five steps

I would come across

you standing at my starting point.

"So long."

. . . Met you again!

"So long."

. . . Met you again!

"So long."

. . . Met you again!

If this is the meaning of "separation"

I like separation. (*Naxie* 130-31)

The global-local interrelatedness in human relationships or the concept of the global village is evoked in the poem "The Fifth Planet of the Little Prince" on people traveling around the globe seeking loved ones. "The Fifth Planet of the Little Prince" is on separation, global travel, and reunion, in my view, and not on the pathos of diaspora or group consciousness of the migrating population. Wan-yu Lin had moved twelve times as of the year 2001 ("Zuwu" 91). "Affected probably by the experience of non-stop moving, I do not have nostalgia for any places to settle down, to wit, the strong and sincere feelings of being forced to leave the hometown or the feelings that make one sleepless" (Wan-yu Lin, "Zuwu" 91).

Another poem "The Second Poem" is on the efficacy of the power of love confronting the dynamism and transformations in this world of globalization and space war:

In this huge, huge

chaotic, chaotic

world where

the elderly are deserted and children die of fathers' abuses.

In this world where

the thing of "liking someone" is too crucial

. . . .

When I like you

I must say it loudly

. . . .

to shake the far and cold star for it to

slightly reposition.

. . . .

Let the numb copy the word "love" again with strokes

tortuous like a labyrinth (Wan-yu Lin, *Naxie* 136-37)

"The Second Poem" suggests that love has the power to move a distant star.

A preceding poem, "With a Poem," suggests that "liking someone" apparently is a trivial matter (Wan-yu Lin, *Naxie* 133):

In this huge, huge

chaotic, chaotic

world where

the elderly are deserted and children die of fathers' abuses.

In this world

the thing of "liking someone" is too trivial

. . . .

Therefore, when I like   you

I must whisper

modestly.

Do not startle the world's open scars

Do not

make the agonizing and the wrathful jealous

. . . .

in an utmost self-reflexive way

. . . .

with a poem. (Wan-yu Lin, *Naxie* 133-35)

From another perspective, "With a Poem" suggests that love can also be personal and not open to the public.

Wan-yu Lin's poetry on globalization and virtual and physical space portrays the accelerating global interconnectedness for two causes including the Internet and global travel. Modern loneliness is more intense and bitter with cyber frauds in virtual space and the commercialization of human relationships in physical space. The global village in physical space is the opposite of secluded lives of modern people in isolation and singleness. Moreover, the low air fares supplied by low-cost carriers and the shortening of travel time by air opened up opportunities of global travel to a larger population. Global travel as Wan-yu Lin's poetry suggests, to a certain degree, is a remedy to the modern problem of solitude.

Other Poets on the Globally Extended

Space: Hsiung Hung, Hsia Yu, and Yin

Ling on the Globetrotter, Space Lag, Nostalgia

for Space, Global Interconnectedness, and Fear

Hsiung Hung on the Globetrotter's Space

Lag and Nostalgia for the Space of Childhood

Also on global travel, the poem "Writing a Poem in Jet Lag" written by Taiwanese woman poet Hsiung Hung and classified as a poem "of old age" in a book of her selected poetry suggests that for a globetrotter suffering from both jet lag and space lag in a foreign country, the unconscious and the space of childhood occupy the mind whereas consciousness and the space of the foreign land are less essential (*Hsiung Hung shi jingxuan*). Likewise,

Wen-Zhi Jian maintains that "the concepts of time and space are diverse" in Hsiung Hung's poetry (63). As her poem "Writing a Poem in Jet Lag" exemplifies, Hsiung Hung writes insightful poems about life in the globally extended space. "Writing a Poem in Jet Lag" has the metaphysical facet indisputably essential to poetry in Hsiung Hung's view. Hsiung Hung maintains that "at a higher level philosophical thoughts confer the significance of beauty" to "sensuous perceptions" in poetry (*Guanyin* 8). Agreeing with Hsiung Hung's view on poetry, Ling Chung maintains that "after 1971" Hsiung Hung's "poetic style tends to be realistic and intellectual" (157).

Hsiung Hung is the pen name of Hu Meizi born in Taitung, Taiwan in 1940 (Yeh and Malmqvist 245). Her book of poetry *Red Coral* (1983) won the Sun Yat-Sen

Literature and Arts Award (Kuei-Yun Lee, "Wenxue" 48 ;

Hsiung Hung, *Guanyin*). Hsiung Hung received a B. A.

from the Department of Fine Arts at National Taiwan

Normal University, an M. A. in Indian Culture at Chinese

Culture University, and a Ph.D. from the Department of

Philosophy at Tunghai University (Kuei-Yun Lee,

"Xiaozhuan" 35). Hsiung Hung is currently retired from

teaching at Tunghai University in Taiwan, at University of

the West in the United States, and at other universities

(Kuei-Yun Lee, "Xiaozhuan" 35).

"Writing a Poem in Jet Lag" examines the two

peculiar phenomena of the narrator during a long-distance

trip to a foreign country—the surfacing of the unconscious

in jet lag and the nostalgia for the space of childhood in

space lag:

A person in jet lag wrote a poem

A person in space lag was pining

In jet lag, the unconscious like a bud poked its head over a trellis,

crept, and spread leaves on the paper to metamorphose into a poem

In space lag, confronting a foreign land's exoticism

a person missed the most ancient and remote childhood, the houses, and

the sea horizon a person sat gazing rhapsodically in childhood

A person in jet lag wrote a poem

A person in space lag was pining

The person did not lag behind

The person was at a yonder corner of the world

May 22, 1998 in Los Angeles (*Hsiung Hung shi jingxuan* 138)

160

Hsiung Hung travelled several times to the United States and could very well have written the poem "Writing a Poem in Jet Lag" during one of her trips to Los Angeles. For example, Hsiung Hung spent Christmas with her husband, son, and daughter-in-law in Los Angeles in 2002 in another trip to the city (Kuei-Yun Lee, *Taiwan* 25). Hsiung Hung visited the University of Iowa in 1974 and taught at University of the West in the United States for a few years (Kuei-Yun Lee, "Xiaozhuan" 35). The sea horizon could allude to the coastline of Taitung where Hsiung Hung grew up as a child and teenager (Kuei-Yun Lee, "Wenxue" 41). As Jing-Yi Chen suggests, "homeland" is one of the three main concerns of Hsiung Hung's poetry in addition to "love" and "Buddhism" (60).

Moreover, the closing of "Writing a Poem in Jet Lag" expounds the feelings of what I call the globetrotter—a traveler journeying to a place on the globe far away from the homeland. "Writing a Poem in Jet Lag" portrays a globetrotter's two unique biological and psychological experiences including desynchronosis and space lag in time-space. The narrator, figuring as a globetrotter in "Writing a Poem in Jet Lag," experiences the inspiration for a poem because the unconscious emerges in jet lag. Space lag, defined as long geographical distance in the poem "Writing a Poem in Jet Lag," makes the narrator wistful for the space of childhood, or the space in the past in the personal time of a person's life. In global travel, the local time of the physical space is not as significant for the globetrotter nostalgic for the space of the past in personal time because the unconscious prevails over consciousness in jet lag, "Writing a Poem in Jet Lag" suggests.

A globetrotter herself, Hsiung Hung travels frequently including a trip to Belgium in 2000 and a journey to Spain in 2004 (Kuei-Yun Lee, *Taiwan* 24-25). Hsiung Hung writes poetry for the reader both near and far from her to share her noumenal ideas and lyric emotions with the reader: "Why do I publish? I think that this is a completion. Writing for myself is no fun. To me, writing for a distant and unknown heart to understand and link with us is a lot of fun" (Ming-Chuan Huang, *Hsiung*). Hsiung Hung suggests that the author and the reader, strangers to one another, are linked by poetry. In a similar vein to this comment by Hsiung Hung, Hsia Yu grapples with the global interconnectedness among strangers in her book of poems *First Person*.

Hsia Yu on the Global Interconnectedness among

Strangers in a Poetics of Interrelatedness and Openness

Taiwanese woman poet Hsia Yu has achieved world fame and currently divides her time between Taipei, Taiwan and Paris, France ("Hsia" 31). In her recent book of poems *First Person* (2016), Hsia Yu writes discerningly on the global interconnectedness among strangers in global space in a poetics of interrelatedness and openness (*First*). On Hsia Yu's "translingualism and transculturalism," not her poetry's reflections on global interconnectivity, J. B. Rollins notes "the openness to alien cultures and languages" in Hsia Yu's poetry (264). I define the poetics of interrelatedness and openness, my coined term, as global interrelatedness, indeterminacy, and experimentality in poetry.

The interrelatedness among strangers and indeterminacy and experimentality in poetry inform the form, poetics, characters, strategies, and subject matter of *First Person*. Global and poetic issues in *First Person* encompass the 2015 terrorist attacks against the employees of the *Charlie Hebdo* magazine and at a kosher supermarket in Paris, France, the disaster of a breach of personal data, and indeterminacy and experimentality in poetry (Meichtry; Moran 316). Other themes are love and loneliness without romance.

The incantatory poetry without titles in *First Person* in both Chinese written by Hsia Yu and English in the translation of Steve Bradbury is printed on unnumbered pages like film subtitles on the bottoms of oftentimes blurred photographs taken by Hsia Yu herself. The book's design without page numbers allows the reader to freely interlink pages into poems or into one long poem. A miniature book ensconced in a frame inside the back cover of *First Person* contains only the poetry in Chinese and English printed on unnumbered pages without photos. The poetry on each page of the miniature book has a long stanza followed by a short stanza.

First Person's postscript suggests: [4]

The design of the book mimics a movie theater showing old movies.

The author hopes that the entwining of poetry and images is regarded as the stills of an unshot movie. (*First*)

In *First Person* Hsia Yu used more than "500 so-called 'bad photographs' taken during her travels and" more than "300 intensely musical phrases" to show "Hsia Yu's obsession with movie/moving images/subtitles/ movie theatre (black box)" ("Hsia" 30). Hsia Yu reprised this strategy in her exhibition *Only Rain Could Make the City Tilt* of "[p]hotographs, poems, and installation" held from November 10, 2018 to January 27, 2019 at Taiwan Contemporary Culture Lab in Taipei ("Hsia" 30-31). The photographs of scenes and people taken during Hsia Yu's travels including the new photos "from her recent northerly travels" intertwined with colorful words of poetry on the bottom ("Hsia" 31). As I saw within the rectangular black structure of the exhibition in 2018, the screen of the photographs and poetry displayed like a movie was located in the end of the structure, and water splattered like rain from the ceiling.

The postscript of *First Person* suggests poetry's indeterminacy:

> For poetry it is like captured clouds
>
> For clouds they will disperse anyway (*First*)

Likewise, in the larger book, the poetry on a photo of two walking people and a sitting person suggests that in *First Person* Hsia Yu's poetics is one of openness:

> The parenthesis opens but always fails to close, poetry and
>
> quantum physics hang in suspense (*First*)

Moreover, the poetry on the page with these two lines in the miniature book portrays the interrelatedness among "strangers," romances, the poetics of openness, and the crowdedness in the metro in summer ("subway") (*First*).

> Likewise, the postscript in verse explains that *First Person*
>
> intends to discuss strangers, poetry, drifting migration, and bad photos.
>
> To bad photos this is a type of blocking
>
> To strangers that is a way to pay respect (*First*)

Furthermore, at the onset *First Person* declares that the character named First Person is vague. The opening of the small book suggests that the reasons for vagueness are differences in time and overlapping photos. The second page in the miniature book opens with the first line in the larger book and has six more lines of poetry:

> First Person emerging from a rocking and swaying and smoke
>
> I don't intend to arrive on time
>
> Showing up ten minutes late is not a good idea in most situations

Have you ever wondered how you'll recognize me?—Well, this is it

By arriving ten minutes late I appear on time for you

Two backlit x-ray photos overlapping

Thus we will meet but why will it seem as though we hadn't?

(*First*)

In the larger book, the first line of poetry in Chinese and its English translation are at the bottom of the photo of a woman walking on the street.

On the fourth page of the miniature book, the second page of poetry in English recounts that Second Person is the next appearing stranger whereas Third Person arrives from the opposite direction:

Second Person divides like fibrous roots

You're very good at being someone one has just come to know

. . . .

Third person is probably approaching from the opposite direction

Is more nebulous and hidden than me, his blood sweat and tears

Is it any wonder he's so fond of seawater too? And so he has all the salt-water there is

(*First*)

The idea underlying Hsia Yu's art exhibition *Only Rain Could Make the City Tilt* could apply to explain her experimental strategy of constructing a network beginning from a sentence and a photo in *First Person*: "Hsia Yu's work begins from a sentence collected, and a snapshot. Much like the horticultural technique of cutting, a sentence can lay down roots, bud, and sprout new branches and leaves" ("Hsia" 30).

171

Furthermore, freedom is a signature trait of Hsia Yu's poetry in subject matter, imagination, and form. Critics such as Fang-ming Chen and I-chih Chen note the freedom in both the ideas and form of Hsia Yu's poetry. In Fang-ming Chen's view, Hsia Yu, an "intellectual poet," expresses her "romanticism," "fantasies, and idealism" in poetry (106). I-chih Chen dubs Hsia Yu "a poet of reveries" as she liberates her language "from the trammels of consciousness to pursue poetic ideas without supervision" (227).

The example *First Person* gives about the valorization of freedom of speech and global interrelatedness in the globally extended space is the attack on the magazine *Charlie Hebdo*'s employees in Paris in 2015 (Moran 316). I ague in Chapter 3 that human rights have three dimensions and are abstract values, national values, and international and global values. Conflicts arose in France because the international and global dimensions of freedom embodied by French ethnic groups or individuals are within the borders of the nation-state that has its own definition of freedom. Freedom of speech and security or the idea of a life without the threats of violence united people and heads of states across national borders though some people in the world disliked the magazine's boldness in certain topics (Meichtry). *First Person* incorporates a photo about a march endorsing freedom of speech as a moment interrelating strangers globally. In this photo in *First Person*, the slogan of "freedom of speech" written in French is in front of a crowd marching on the street. Some words of the slogan are blocked by a man in front of the camera. The couplet on this page is about seawater and salty water:

Is it any wonder he's so fond of seawater too?

And so he has all the salt-water there is (*First*)

This couplet in the larger book is the last line of the couplet on the fourth page in the small book. Third Person in the poetry corresponds with the person blocking the slogan in the photo. The blocking by the man of some of the words of the slogan reminds us in a poetics of openness that the relationship between the photos and the poetry is not a fixed one. The explanation in the brochure of Hsia Yu's exhibition *Only Rain Could Make the City Tilt* also alerts the reader to this freedom in her work that destabilizes any invariable relationships between the photos and the poetry:

"The photographs might not always match the poetry, just like subtitles do not always reflect what is playing on the screen as image and text become juxtaposed into an altogether different message" ("Hsia" 31). In other words, for Hsia Yu, freedom is also an abstract value in the first dimension I postulate.

To the left of the page with a photo about freedom of speech is a photo of the head of the sculpture of a man. The poetry on this page to the left is about salty bodily fluids flowing in injuries, work, and sorrow:

Is more nebulous and hidden than me, his blood sweat and tears

(*First*)

This line on the photo of the sculpture is also the first line of the couplet on the fourth page of the miniature book.

Later in *First Person,* in a poetics of openness the narrator explains the blocking of words and the blurring of photos:

I wonder how, from the rain, you can recognize the rain,

From the snow the snow, from the word the word (*First*)

As foreshadowed in the photo of the marching people and the poetry hinting at wounds, toiling, and pang, the postscript suggests that the songs in *First Person* are "elegies" for tragic incidents such as the attack on the magazine and the kosher supermarket:

Poetry is love poetry the songs are elegies the photos are bad photos

(*First*)

Songs symbolize the interrelatedness among strangers in life:

Look at these strangers coming toward us—can this be my Greek chorus?

. . . .

Like a perfect stranger so easily replaced

So easily replaced by yet another stranger waiting to be replaced and so again they

come and go (*First*)

In addition to freedom, a central concern of *First Person* is the risks in global interconnectedness in virtual space. On two pages with a photo of people on the metro or a bus, the poetry suggests that by confessing online and exposing their personal lives in cyberspace people run the risk of allowing a large number of people access to their scandals. The poetry on a page in the miniature book points out the concomitance between global interconnectedness and risks:

177

A text message made of ten thousand phrases is like ten thousand little fish

When ten thousand little fish are swimming together they will suddenly turn tail and

move in the opposite direction

A single fish does not a contradiction make but ten thousand fish just might

Don't you see that during the day, at any given moment, there are tens of thousands

of strangers in these underground passages

The divulgence of personal data about tens of thousands of people does little to

hinder them from washing their dirty laundry together

Proving the opacity of the one does little to impede the transparency of the whole

Proving the opacity of the whole does little to impede the transparency of the one

(*First*)

Benjamin Clark detects "cynicism and dread" in Hsia Yu's love poems, while *First Person* chronicles risks (98). *First Person* explores global interconnectedness among strangers and their choices to stay united or connected despite risks of attacks and personal data breaches.

The relationships among strangers on Earth are like the relationships among the pages of poetry in *First Person*. The pages can freely interrelate, written and devised in a poetics of interrelatedness and openness. The miniature book of *First Person* gives a regular form to the poetry. By contrast, the poetry in the larger book resonates among the pages as poems or a poem. In her poetry, Yin Ling dwells on global politics more explicitly than Hsia Yu. The next section will discuss Yin Ling's poem "A White Dove Flew Over" on global politics, fear, and freedom.

Yin Ling on Fear, Wars, and Global

Politics in the Globally Extended Space

Yin Ling's poem "A White Dove Flew Over" chronicles the moments when space is extended; the significance and practice of freedom are in flux and are transformed more by global politics than by the nation-state. My three dimensions of human rights as abstract values, national values, and international and global values are fully presented in "A White Dove Flew Over." Moreover, to Ying Ling, as the poem "A White Dove Flew Over" suggests, fear is the emotion modern people have about global politics and wars in the globally extended space. Yin Ling's poem "A White Dove Flew Over" anthologized in a transnational anthology of women's poetry written in Chinese, *Thirty Women Poets on Two*

180

Shores, examines the polemic of global politics in matters of peace and war in the globally extended space. "A White Dove Flew Over" suggests that global politics can negotiate peace for people in a distant nation-state in war, but there is a difference between negotiated peace, such as truce or a peace agreement, and real peace.

Global politics can shape the destiny of a nation and the fate of its people. For example, the Bosnian war ended in 1995 with the signing of the Dayton accords in Paris (Campbell 153-54). By contrast, global politics did not bring about true peace for people in South Vietnam as in the example of the New Year battle. The battle broke out in South Vietnam in 1968 despite a truce agreement (Ming-Chuan Huang, *Yin Ling* 1). In the globally extended space, global politics restored peace in Bosnia but not in

Vietnam. The poem "A White Dove Flew Over" on global politics in the globally extended space suggests that global politics may mediate peace but cannot guarantee peace and freedom in the globally extended space.

"A White Dove Flew Over" portrays the globally extended space with its two descriptors, heterogeneity in composition and deterritorialization in my first haecceitic dimension. The space where global politics is extremely involved such as Vietnam is multiscalar, heterogeneous, and deterritorializing. The space of Vietnam in war was multiscalar because it was both local and global, and was heterogeneous because the space was defined simultaneously by the Vietnamese and parties of global politics. Moreover, the space of Vietnam for Yin Ling and in her poem "A White Dove Flew Over" is deterritorialized without reterritorialization because the homeland South Vietnam does not exist anymore.

Yin Ling's education in three nations, travels across the world, migration, and binational self-identity make her one of the Taiwanese poets writing finely etched poems on global themes. Yin Ling herself recognizes that in both her "life and writings undecidedness, roaming, and grief for a long time have had extremely important roles" (Ha 292). Yin Ling is the first name of Ha Kim-lan born in Mỹ Tho, Vietnam in 1945 (Yin Ling, Interview; "Ha"; Yin Ling, "Piaopo"; Ming-Chuan Huang, *Yin Ling*). Yin Ling left Vietnam in 1969 to enroll at National Taiwan University where she received an M.A. and a Ph.D. degree in Chinese literature (Ming-Chuan Huang, *Yin Ling* 1). After teaching at Tamkang University in Taiwan for two years, Yin Ling left Taiwan for Paris in 1979 to pursue her Ph.D. studies at University of Paris VII and received a Ph.D. degree in 1984 (Yin Ling, Interview; Ming-Chuan Huang, *Yin Ling* 1). Yin Ling returned to Vietnam several times in the middle of and after her studies abroad in 1971, 1973, 1994, and later (Ming-Chuan Huang, *Yin Ling* 1; Yin Ling, "Zi" 191). After she received a Ph.D. degree from University of Paris VII, Yin Ling taught at Tamkang University in Taiwan and currently is Honorary Professor in the Department of Chinese Literature (Ming-Chuan Huang, *Yin Ling* 1; "Ha").

Yin Ling loves to travel and composes poetry drawing on materials from her journeys all over the world: "The influences and so forth of different nations and cultures on me are certainly immensely helpful in writing," says Yin Ling (Ming-Chuan Huang, *Yin Ling* 1). Yin Ling says in an interview that she "often travels alone" and sometimes with her daughter "to understand and explore another culture and another world" (qtd. in Tzu Chuan 241, 248-49). Indeed, in my view, Yin Ling's poetry demonstrates the merits of global consciousness and a modern mind. As Hui-Chien Ku suggests, Yin Ling has the generous mind of a cosmopolitan (11). Moreover, in my view, Yin Ling's imagery on most occasions has the stark beauty of simplicity. The poem "A White Dove Flew Over" is a lapidary example.

As a writer, Yin Ling has a binational self-identity. Yin Ling sees herself as a Vietnamese writer in the first half of her life and a Taiwanese writer in the second half of her life after she became a naturalized Taiwanese citizen by marriage (Yin Ling, Interview). For some Taiwanese critics, Yin Ling is a Vietnamese poet or a poet with the "diasporic" "experience of migration" (Wan-Yun Hsia 45; Ku 13). Moreover, on Yin Ling's cultural mooring, Shu-ling Horng notes that Yin Ling has the "consciousness of vagrancy" (195).

Yin Ling's poem "A White Dove Flew Over" at the onset contrasts the magnificent palace of France with the ice-covered and war-ravaged Sarajevo where civilians died. War did not desist but raged on:

Forever

irrelevant people

thousands of kilometers away (such as Paris)

in a lofty palace (such as the Élysée Palace)

sealed your fate

your life or death in the future,

signing what they call

a contract,

a nuisance ("A" 213)

Yin Ling disapproves of any peace agreements without real peace. The poem "A White Dove Flew Over" draws both from a news story Yin Ling learned about in Paris and from her memories of wars in Vietnam (Ming-Chuan Huang, *Yin Ling* 2). Yin Ling, a woman poet born in Vietnam and immigrating to Taiwan, composed "A White Dove Flew Over" on April 22, 1996 (*A White* 31). While in Paris from July 1995 to February 1996, Yin Ling knew from the news that a peace agreement was signed at the

Élysée Palace, the office of the French president, in Paris in 1995, yet war in Sarajevo dragged on (Ming-Chuan Huang, *Yin Ling* 2). At that moment, Yin Ling recalled, "all the bitter memories about Vietnam flooded back" (Ming-Chuan Huang, *Yin Ling* 2). Yin Ling remembered that just as for Sarajevo in Paris in 1995, peace agreements for South Vietnam were signed in Geneva in 1954 (Ming-Chuan Huang, *Yin Ling* 2). The Vietminh still waged war on South Vietnam after the Geneva agreements sliced Vietnam into North Vietnam and South Vietnam in 1954 (Holmes and Matrix Evans 326). "Symbolically, we signed an agreement," but the agreement did not make peace, Yin Ling said (Ming-Chuan Huang, *Yin Ling* 2). "On this account, would peace truly arrive? In reality, no. A white dove of peace chanced to fly past only," comments

Yin Ling on peace agreements (qtd. in Tzu Chuan 242).

Yin Ling remembered that the civil war of Vietnam

erupted in 1954 (qtd. in Tzu Chuan 237). In another

example, Yin Ling recalled that though a truce was signed,

North Vietnam broke the cease-fire in 1968 by attacking

South Vietnam (Ming-Chuan Huang, *Yin Ling* 1). "North

Vietnamese and Vietcong" took "advantage of a truce"

during the New Year holidays (Holmes and Matrix Evans

329).

Yin Ling was upset because peace agreements did not

bring Vietnam peace. Just as Bai Ling and other scholars

suggest, the apodictic telos of the critique of war in the

poem "A White Dove Flew Over" is the Vietnam War

("Qizai" 20). Like Bai Ling, Wan-Yun Hsia and other

scholars maintain that "A White Dove Flew Over" hints at

the Vietnam War by writing about the Bosnian war (24).

Signed in Paris on December 14, 1995, the Dayton accords

ended the Bosnian war, achieved peace, and divided the

land into two nation-states, the Republika Srpska and the

Federation of Bosnia and Herzegovina (Campbell 153-54;

Ramet 80; Harsch 38-39).

The second stanza recounts the news about a family

Yin Ling learned of in Paris (Ming-Chuan Huang, *Yin Ling*

2). All the male members of the family fought in the

Bosnian war, leaving a child at home who was killed by a

bullet (Ming-Chuan Huang, *Yin Ling* 2). When the Dayton

accords were signed in Paris, Sarajevo was in snow and

war, Yin Ling recalled (Ming-Chuan Huang, *Yin Ling* 2):

You certainly were still on your own land

covered by ice and snow

Your heart was stiff and froze

The only child left at home

yesterday in a none-of-his-business

conflict between two parties

was hit by a

bullet

just delivered ("A" 213-14)

The second stanza illustrates Yin Ling's mission to be the spokesperson for civilians in her poems on wars. Yin Ling suggests that her war poems register "the voices of civilians": "I wrote about the voices of the pitiable people from the lowest class in society" (Ming-Chuan Huang, *Yin Ling* 2). More than one critic opines that humanitarianism underpins Yin Lin's poetry. For example, Ruwen Ren suggests that Yin Ling's poetry throughout her career shows "the spirit of humanitarianism from the stance of civilians" (3). Agreeing with Ruwen Ren, Jung Tzu maintains that Yin Ling's poetry is informed by her "concerns on the reality of humanity and true experience of survival" (12). Likewise, to Ku, Yin Ling's poetry "is expressive of her care and affection for the human world" (11).

A humanitarian poet, Yin Ling declares that poetry must have both social value and beauty: "The most ideal poetry of the highest level ought to have the artistic beauty of poetry as well as concerns about society and life" ("Lun shige" 128). In a similar comment, Wen-Chen Chen maintains that her poems have the "qualities and characteristics of both lyric and epic poems" (67).

Likewise, Jian-Long Yang suggests from another vantage point that Yin Ling's style is both "heavy and nimble" (98).

The last stanza ends with an image of a white dove flying in the snow-covered capital of Bosnia, Sarajevo. The dove, a symbol of peace, is injured because by chance it flies over Sarajevo in war:

Snow still drifted in Sarajevo

Holding an icicle of blood in its beak

that white dove

it

just chanced to

fly

over ("A" 214)

Yin Ling's later poem "Years of Bewilderment" suggests further that the white dove is an image of peace in her poetry:

> We read *War and Peace*
>
> endeavoring to find a real white dove which had not lost its way
>
> in the midst of ceaseless warfare and bombs
>
> (*Yin Ling jieju* 106)

Wen-Chen Chen maintains that the "innocent" dove in the poem "A White Dove Flew Over" is sacrificed because it flew over the capital in war (56). The dove's wound in the closing of the poem is foreshadowed in the second stanza by the child's death. As Yin Ling suggested in an interview in 2019, the dove is only injured but not killed (Interview). Like the white dove injured for fluttering in the war zone by chance, Vietnamese people were wounded or died because their nation was in war at that moment.

Yin Ling's poem "A White Dove Flew Over" suggests that in the globally extended space, global politics determines peace, war, the destiny of a faraway nation-state, and people's fate. In its litany for real peace, Yin Ling's poem "A White Dove Flew Over" nevertheless adumbrates that fear is the emotion modern people feel about wars and global politics. Yin Ling said in an interview in 2019 that fearing that communists would appear right before her eyes, she had been unable to sleep well after the New Year of 1968 (Interview).

Ideas of Space in Taiwanese Poetry on
the Globally Extended Space after the 1950s

In Taiwanese poetry on the globally extended space published after the 1950s I examine in this chapter, the globally extended space is affective in Chou-yu Cheng's poem "Celeste Sky." The globally extended space is also deterritorializing, for example, in Chou-yu Cheng's poems "The Eternity of Václavské Square," "You Did Not Return from the Trip," "Three United States of America," Wan-yu Lin's poems "Solitude is Real" and "The Fifth Planet of the Little Prince," Hsia Yu's book of poems *First Person*, and Yin Ling's poem "A White Dove Flew Over." Moreover, the globally extended space is related and affective in both Wan-yu Lin's poetry and Hsiung Hung's poem "Writing a Poem in Jet Lag." In both Wan-yu Lin's and Hsia Yu's poetry, the globally extended space is interrelated and virtual.

Furthermore, Chou-yu Cheng's two poems on freedom, "The Eternity of Václavské Square" and "You Did Not Return from the Trip," substantiate my theory in Chapter 3 that the extension of space redefines or ensures human freedom. Yin Ling's poem "A White Dove Flew Over" verifies my theory in the third chapter that the extension of space redefines human rights including freedom, in this case more by global politics than by nation-states. Chou-yu Cheng's, Hsia Yu's, and Yin Ling's poetry on freedom sets out all three of my dimensions of freedom as an abstract value, a national value, and an international and global value.

Conclusion

Taiwanese poetry on the globally extended space published after the 1950s attests to a confluence of issues including freedom, territoriality, nostalgia for space, solitude, global travel, interconnectedness, and fear. In the panoply of poems on the globally extended space published by Taiwanese poets after the 1950s, Chou-yu Cheng's poetry valorizes freedom with global examples and expatiates on three issues concerned with the nation-state's territoriality in the globally extended space including sojourning, national security, and diaspora. His poetry also testifies to the authority of the borders of the nation-state and deciphers nostalgia as pining for territories and for cultural and linguistic heritages. The poetry of Wan-yu Lin and Hsia Yu suggests that the Internet, capitalism, and global travel further global interconnectivity. Wan-yu Lin's poetry ponders the deepening of loneliness by frauds in cyberspace and the commercialization of human relationships in both cyberspace and physical space and the abating of solitude by global travel. Hsia Yu's poetry collection *First Person* in a poetics of interrelatedness and openness illuminates the global interconnectedness among strangers and among words in their prodigious encounters in the globally extended space.

Hsiung Hung's poem "Writing a Poem in Jet Lag" registers the dominance of the unconscious in jet lag and the domination of the space of childhood in space lag for a globetrotter or long-distance traveler. Finally, safety is one of the issues of paramount importance in globalization. A great amount of recent scholarship on safety in the globally extended space attests to the fact that safety is one of the top priorities for modern people and nation-states. Chou-yu Cheng's poem "Three United States of America" and Yin Ling's poem "A White Dove Flew Over" suggest that national security and fear are two issues in the globally extended space in globalization. Yin Ling's poem "A White Dove Flew Over" intimates that in the globally extended space human rights including freedom are defined more by global politics than by the nation-state.

In spatial concepts, Taiwanese poetry on the globally extended space examined in this chapter portrays the globally extended space to be affective and deter-ritorializing in its relatedness and interrelatedness.

Deterritorialization is one of the two descriptors of my first haecceitic dimension of space. The relatedness of space and the affective secondary dimension of space are represented in Wan-yu Lin's poem "Solitude is Real" on solitude and Hsiung Hung's poem "Writing a Poem in Jet Lag" on the globetrotter. Interrelatedness in the globally extended space in the social and international dimension and in the virtual secondary dimension of space is the theme of Wan-yu Lin's poems "Solitude is Real" and "The Fifth Planet of the Little Prince" and Hsia Yu's book of poems *First Person*.

Moreover, Chou-yu Cheng's two poems on freedom, "The Eternity of Václavské Square" and "You Did Not Return from the Trip," prove my theory in the third chapter that the extension of space redefines or preserves human freedom. Additionally, Yin Ling's poem "A White Dove Flew Over" confirms my theory in Chapter 3 that human rights including freedom in certain instances are transformed more by global politics than by nation-states. Finally, Chou-yu Cheng's, Hsia Yu's, and Yin Ling's poetry on freedom has amply demonstrated all three of my dimensions of freedom as an abstract value, a national value, and an international and global value. Wan-yu Lin's and Hsia Yu's poetry also explores global interconnectedness in our lives today. In chapters 5 and 6, I will examine the works on global interrelatedness written by two American poets Graham and Bei Dao.

Chapter 5

Jorie Graham's Poetics of Interrelatedness

Introduction: Poetics of

Interrelatedness and Globalization

In a keen awareness of our interconnectedness, Graham embraces a poetics of interrelatedness, my coined term. I define a poetics of interrelatedness as a view of the self in poetry as interconnected with others. The poetics of interrelatedness suggests people's interconnectedness within the context of globalization captured in modern poetry. With a global awareness, as this chapter illuminates, we can appreciate with even greater acuity literature's achievements in its forms and thoughts as well as the linguistic liaison and cultural connectivity Lisa Lowe, Stuart Hall, and other critics suggest (Lowe 11, 37; Hall

176, 183-84; qtd. in MacCabe 40). Our indisputable literary global interrelatedness and perviousness manifest in this examination. One realizes that national and cultural boundaries and what Samuel Huntington calls "the fault lines between civilizations" cannot crimp the reading and writing of literature when one considers both the liaison between Graham's poem "Event Horizon" and Bei Dao's poem "Daydream" and the fact that other contemporary poets cite as their influences poets such as Paul Celan, Du Fu, Rainer Maria Rilke, and Charles Baudelaire and rhapsodize about these international luminaries (29). In the expressions of this sense of interrelatedness, Graham comments on both the power and disempowerment of global media in "Event Horizon," citing two lines from Bei Dao's poem "Daydream." For Graham, the globally extended space is interrelated. In her poems on global media and communication technologies, the globally extended space in the social and international dimension is interrelated. Moreover, Graham's poem "Event Horizon" portrays human rights as abstract values for their universality and as international and global values that are defined and sempiternally redefined by the viewers of global media.

Global Media, Graham's Poetics of Interrelatedness, and the Othering of Place

Employing the theory of Giddens on trust, this paper argues that in her poem "Event Horizon" Graham explores and constructs the global interconnectedness among people in this age in a poetics of interrelatedness. Global denizens' interconnected absences, our intimate strangeness to each other, make trust indispensable in the coordination of global affairs. On interrelatedness, Graham maintains that human beings now must have a sense of themselves as a species in a global-minded cosmopolitanism owing to our interdependency and, therefore, interrelatedness:

> So part of what we need to do at this point, with the imagination, is help people imagine what it is like to be part of a species, and what it is like to be on one planet, and what it is like to be interdependent with other people. ("America's").

Graham's poetics of interrelatedness explains her selection of poetry when she assumes the position of an editor. David Lehman was impressed "by her profoundly ecumenical taste" as guest editor of *The Best American Poetry 1990* (8).

In a plotline primarily concerned with a woman who washes a stain off a red dress outside on a wintry day, while on TV an anchor reads news about the Tiananmen Square demonstration, Graham offers up a view on global interconnectedness. In stanzaic form, the poem renovates the tradition of the long line by enlisting the form of the verse paragraph—indenting the first line of a group of lines on an action or a theme and capitalizing the first letter of the first line—to clarify the plot of a poem. Just as Stephen Burt maintains, Graham's zigzagging long line befits ideationally her overall fondness for openness: "Graham's irregular, often very long lines represent self-revision and inconclusiveness in thought" (1147). The poem's speaker, the woman washing out the stain, has an epiphany about one's global interrelatedness mediated as it is by the media during the Tiananmen Square Tragedy in 1989. "Event Horizon" culminates in a skeptical stance toward the media that we nevertheless have to trust and inconsolable grief for the Tiananmen Square Tragedy:

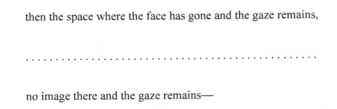

then the space where the face has gone and the gaze remains,

. . . .

no image there and the gaze remains—

no place there and the gaze remains— (*Materialism* 54)

Critics including Thomas Gardner and Kathy-Ann Tan render this ethical epistemology as a grasp of "the limits of knowing" and "limits of human knowledge," respectively (Gardner 125; Tan 99).

"Event Horizon" registers what Giddens calls "active trust," "trust in which there is two-way negotiation and regular monitoring" of "the integrity of the other," and that "has to be consistently renewed" in "an open form of life" in this age of globalization owing to global denizens' interconnectivity (*Europe* 115-16, xi). "Event Horizon" reflects on the global media that one is obliged by circumstances, and not by reason, to trust (Giddens, *Modernity* 23). Global media could subserve as an example of "expert systems," one of the two types of "*abstract systems*" according to Giddens, who defines expert systems as "systems of technical accomplishment or professional expertise that organise large areas of the material and social environments" and depend "on rules of procedure transferable from individual to individual" (*Consequences* 27, 80 and *Modernity* 243). As a child, Graham was a constituent of global media and was familiar with its operations of which trust is an issue. While she was a child in Rome, Graham was surrounded by both news and art as her father Curtis Bill Pepper, "a foreign correspondent" stationed in Italy, and her mother Beverly Pepper, "a painter and sculptor," had an office and a studio in the house (Hevesi 19; "Under"). In Rome Graham lived within a sphere of news because her father became the bureau chief of *Newsweek* in Rome in 1956, and her father and the media conglomerate had to trust

Graham, a young child at that time, in relaying the news, and so must the reading public:

> Dictated cables came in from my father at crazy hours from the Belgian Congo or the Middle East that I was designated to transcribe and transmit, beginning at age 8, to news headquarters in the States. ("Under"; Hevesi 19)

On the exceptional presence of news in Graham's life and poetry, Jahan Ramazani comments:

> Graham also grew up in a period of increasing news saturation, and part of her achievement, too, has been to develop inventive strategies for negotiating the relations between poetry and the news, between private experience and global public history. (121)

If "Event Horizon" inexorably impels us to see that trust is de rigueur for the subsistence of global media in this age of globalization and to grasp the media's confines, Graham's poem "Later in Life" about a call "without dissipation or dilation" from a worker on the ground to another worker "on / the seventh floor" one summer concerns the inviolate conveyance of messages as Graham explains:

> It's also a kind of *ars poetica* because it is a poem about the utopian dream of perfect communication between one individual and another. . . . But the dream of poetry is that someone writing a poem in the 1100s would be, if I read it today, speaking to me directly and as intimately as if I were standing before them. (*Sea*, 19; "Later")

In the poem, next, when "the anchorman's back," he announces that the viewers could not see live scenes owing to the loss of satellite signals, so that all the viewers can see is "the anchor's face" (*Materialism* 52):

> and all we get is the anchor's face
>
>> and sometimes voice-over onto the freeze-frame
>
> where coverage
>
>> was interrupted. (*Materialism* 52)

Indeed, an event horizon delimits the "boundary of a black hole . . . where the escape velocity" equals that of "the speed of light," and beyond which "no information can reach" the outside observer ("Event"; Morris 151-52).

Graham turns her gaze back on herself, exploring one's trust in global media sustained by the "*faceless commitments*" of global media (*Consequences* 80). Giddens demarcates two sorts of commitments that undergird a trust relationship—"*facework commitments*" and "*faceless commitments*," with the former built on personal contact and presence, and the latter facilitated through "*abstract systems*" with the parties absent (*Consequences* 80). For trust to be built, both faceless and facework commitments are at work at the "access points" "between lay individuals or collectivities and the representatives of abstract systems" (Giddens, *Consequences* 83, 88). Giddens suggests that the access point, where trust is gained, is the vulnerable spot of an abstract system, and in the poem, the trustworthiness of the expert system, global media, is put to the test during the hiatus of satellite pictures (*Consequences* 88, 91). "Event Horizon" likens the anchor's face to the stain on the woman's dress, an index to an event occurring at another time (*Materialism* 52).

This mesmerization of the narrator of "Event Horizon" by a massacre on the other side of the globe testifies to the interrelatedness of us. Place in this epoch metamorphoses into what I call "prodigal place" profuse with other loci and times through the instant transmission of information as well as media-shaped and memory-suffused experience. The othering of place arises from the presence of the absent other in the site of one's physical presence (Giddens, *Modernity* 187). Néstor García Canclini defines globalization as the complex interplays of nation-states, businesses, and people in "a segmented and unequal process": "globalization is imagined as the copresence and interaction of all countries, of all corporations, and all consumers" (151). Graham remarks on our interconnectedness through communication technology:

> I think that perhaps we are trying to keep ourselves more human by being in touch a great deal. Certainly, what I find very interesting is the global community growing able to instantaneously share a similar image via the internet. ("How Has")

To Claudia Rankine, Graham's poetry is attentive to both relations and presence: "Jorie Graham's masterful poems traverse almost four decades of inquiry into what it means to be in relation. . . . [H]er fifteen collections have built towards a brilliant insistence on presence" ("The American" 11). Willard Spiegelman also suggests that as she grows into a major American poet, Graham "has also moved from being an art and culture poet to a political and philosophical one" (1098). "Event Horizon" captures a woman's moment of global civic consciousness in the othering of place.

Place is a crucial element of Graham's poetry. Graham comments on the place in a poem as a turning point:

And although it is, most traditionally, a literal place . . . often, too, a historical "moment"— especially the very conflagatory "now" of one's historical-yet-subjective existence—is felt as a location that compels action, reaction, and the sort of re-equilibration which a poem seeks. A break in the comprehensible, in the morally absorbable—a fissure in the spirit's sense of just cause and effect, in a line of thought that can feel "true"—can constitute trigger-occasions, or situations, or kinds of place from which the spirit in language springs forward into the action of poetry. All such moments—where we are taken by surprise and asked to react—are marked places in consciousness, places where a "turn" is required. ("Something" 7)

Graham's poem "Event Horizon" illuminates the othering of place during the Tiananmen Square Tragedy in 1989. A parenthetical dedication under the title of "Event Horizon" indicates that the poem is "[f]or Bei-Dao, June 1989" (*Materialism* 50). The notes of the book *Materialism* credit two lines of quotes from Bei Dao's "Daydream" (*Materialism* 145):

A crack has appeared between day and night writes

Bei Dao,

and *you did not get back at the time we*

appointed. (*Materialism* 52)

The rupture in time serves as an omen for the massacre in Tiananmen Square, while the entrance into a phase of democracy was forestalled. "Event Horizon" gives a caveat about the violation of freedom by alluding to Hans Andersen's fairytale "The Red Shoes." "Event Horizon" compares the divestment of freedom to a fixed coupling of accouterment with the body, contrasted with the freedom to change the outfits, connoted by "the flapping thrumming dress all / sleeves of wind" worn by no one (Andersen 110; *Materialism* 54). "Event Horizon" is indebted to Wallace Stevens's poem "The Idea of Order at Key West," as Catherine Sona Karagueuzian points out: "The water never formed to mind or voice, / Like a body wholly body, fluttering / Its empty sleeves" (Karagueuzian 15; Stevens 128). In "The Idea of Order at Key West," new meanings of the world accrue from the song: "It was her voice that made / The sky acutest at its vanishing" (Karagueuzian 15; Stevens 129). "Event Horizon" and Graham's other poems instead focalize on "doomed outsideness of me" in the lyric, the separation of one's subjective activities from the physical world (Karagueuzian 15; *Materialism* 54; Graham, "My" 22). Graham defends the concept of the self and treats "the unyielding boundary between self and other" in her poetry as Nikki Skillman suggests (207, 226-27, 210). Kylan Rice also suggests that Graham's "poetry harps on the fear that the gap between the real and the experience of the real cannot be bridged" (97). Like Rice, Sarah Ehlers maintains that in Graham's poetry "a gap opens between history and representation—between the real of history and real of a self in history" (29).

Likewise, because of a stance on the constraints of one's perception, Graham's poem "Event Horizon" suggests that a person's interpretation of a historical incident, others, or the world approximates beauty rather than truth. The poem mourns the protesters who died at Tiananmen Square fighting for freedom embodied by the statue of the Goddess of Democracy erected in the square (Feng 449). The speaker interrelates the goddess and

Helen of Troy, whose "living face" is like "a stain on the flames" of the burning city (*Materialism* 54):

> among the folds of radio signals, hovering, translucent
>
> inside the dress of fizzing, clicking golden
>
> frequencies—the pale, invisible flames—
>
> is the face of the most beautiful woman in the world
>
> (*Materialism* 54)

With a title about Graham's target audience, a later poem, "Posterity," as "Event Horizon" does, reveals that for Graham, a poem's telos is to immortalize beauty through versification ("to lift the subject to a place of beauty," and to "make of the grief a kind of beauty that might / endure") (*Overlord* 88, 86).

Finally, the globally extended space is interrelated for Graham. The globally extended space is interrelated because global media in her poem "Event Horizon" focalizes on the linking of viewers around the world. Moreover, human rights are abstract values because of the universality of these rights. Human rights are international and global values because global media and the Internet allow global denizens to judge together and exchange the definitions of human rights.

Conclusion: Interrelatedness

In life, Graham globally supports free speech. In 2016, in an open letter she and other writers appealed for the release of Palestinian poet Dareen Tatour arrested for the poetry she wrote ("Poetry"). Furthermore, Graham's poem "Swarm" portrays emotional proximity and interconnection among people realized by communication technology ("this tiny geometric swarm of / openings") in this globalized world (*Swarm* 58). In addition to treating subject matter of global scale such as global media and communication, Graham's poetry has transnational viability, verified with the International Nonino Prize she received from Italy in 2013 and with the Forward Prize she earned from the U.K. and Ireland in 2012 ("Nonino"; "Jorie Graham Wins"; "Forward"). In our interrelatedness, poetry matters globally. In chapter 6, I will discuss Bei Dao's works on the global interrelatedness of literature and universal subjectivity.

Chapter 6

Globalization and Universal Subjectivity in Bei Dao's "Daydream"

Introduction: Globalization and Universal Subjectivity

Bei Dao's idea of globalization exemplifies the interrelatedness of literature. Moreover, on the self-other relationship and our connectedness, the epiphany in his poem "Daydream" illuminates Fichte's concept of humans as free and rational beings and, out of a respect for others, proposes a universal subjectivity. Furthermore, to Bei Dao, the globally extended space is deterritorializing.

Bei Dao as a Poet, His Style, and His Critics

As in Graham's poetry, interrelatedness is intriguingly present in Bei Dao's work. In a larger context, in this section I offer a critical evaluation of Bei Dao's position in literary history, his work's aesthetic value, his poetry's style, as well as content, and next compare the poet's self-image and poetics with the poet as seen by his critics. One of the major post-Cultural Revolution Chinese poets and now an American poet, Bei Dao composes poetry on the sublime and loss in addition to other themes. I maintain that his work espouses individualism, collectivism, universalism, and optimism within pessimism. Moreover, Bei Dao employs the techniques of dissociation and advances intensity, transcendence, and animosity in poetry. Intricate poetry, universalism, and animosity in his poetry make Bei Dao a globally esteemed poet quoted by Graham and myriad other writers and people.

Literary History and Aesthetic Value:

The Sublime after the Cultural Revolution

Bei Dao occupies an indisputable position in modern Chinese literature for his participation in a post-Cultural Revolution poetry magazine *Today* that reacted against the dominance of official discourse. The aesthetic value of Bei Dao's poetry is to a great extent founded on a deft deployment of diction carefully chosen to attain the purpose of the sublime. In his poetry, Bei Dao creates both a spatial sense of "vastness" and a continuum in time—a timeless time waiting to be defined and explicated (Pozzana 93). On his poem "The Answer," Qin Li argues likewise that his imagery "is prone toward 'magnitude' " (17).[1]

Styles and Content: Individualism, Collectivism, Univer-

sality, the Tragedy with Openings, Loss, and Dissociation

Bei Dao writes in a self-oriented style of poetry that "places much emphasis on poetry's accommodating capacity, the unconscious, and the capturing of the perception of an instant" (Bei Dao, "Wo" 90). This style yields "a highly individualized" language that gives emphasis to the "expressivity" of "the poetic language" (Ying 10; Janssen 262; Bei Dao, "A Note"). A trait that demarcates his poetry from that of many of his contemporaries' writings in other countries is that while his poems champion individualism, they always carry collective implications and appeal explicitly to universal values sonorously pleaded by his speakers. For example,

"Daydream" suggests that its narrating voice can refer to the self as well as the collective "we":

The noses that collect dust

touched each other and

kept talking: this is I

is I

I, we (*Bei Dao* 174)

In agreement with the first half of my view on individualism, Michelle Yeh's remark about the works of poets who publish in *Today* can aptly apply to Bei Dao's poetry as well: the poetry "bespeaks a quest of individualism in a collectivist society, a quest of meaning in an age of darkness" (52). Likewise, Qin Li comments on the heroic romanticism, intended as a strain of individualism, in Bei Dao's poem "The Answer." "The Answer" "abounds with a touch of heroism and sentiments of romanticism," Qin Li suggests (17). Concurring with the first half of my statement, Yongguo Chen maintains that "[t]he history of the obscurists . . . is loosely the history of how modern Chinese poets tried to regain the identity and subjectivity as human beings," though to Chen the "collectivity" in this poetry is grounded more in sociohistorical reality than its universality: "The experience of social upheaval and personal destiny determines the obscurists' perspective, which is solipsistic with a spirit of collectivity" (93-95).

The tour de force of Bei Dao, "a tragic poet" dubbed by Wen Zhong, rests in his poetry's dramatization of what I call "the tragedy with openings," portraying the intransigent will of a defiant individual defending, in adverse circumstances, the value and the dignity of human existence (78). Zicheng Hong perceives the tragicalness as an "internal conflict," while Chien Chang puts it as an act to "oscillate eternally among hopes, crises, and disappointment (and even despair)" (Hong 348; Chang, *Qing* 260). Bei Dao interprets the optimism within pessimism when he describes the world he constructs in poetry: "a poet should establish a world of his own. This is a sincere and unique world, a righteous world, and a world of justice and humanity" ("Wo" 90). Myriad critics also comment about "idealism," "love and humanity," "humanism," and skepticism in Bei Dao's poetry, but none has explored the idea of tragedy with a futuristic tendency and hopes in his poetry (Luo 197-98, 200; Hong 348; Niu

7; Guang-wei Cheng 177). In addition to tragicalness, loss is the mood that dominates the poet's life: "since youth, I have lived in loss: the loss of belief, the loss of one's amour, the loss of language, and so forth. Through writing, I search for directions" (qtd. in Tang 69).

Befitting his poetry's pervasive atmosphere of loss is the dissociation of the objects from their referents in the images and occurrences that his poems describe, a "disjunctive mode of expressions" for Isabella Wai, inspired by cinematography as related by Bei Dao:

> I essay to introduce the cinematic technique of montage into my own poetry to produce collision among images and swift switches so as to spur people's imagination to fill in the blanks left by wide leaps. (Wai 184; Bei Dao, "Wo" 90)

Agreeing with this remark, Ru-Shan Song suggests that leaps are one of the techniques Misty poets adopt (36). Objects and occurrences in his poetry are uprooted from their contexts because of the absence of explanatory linkages between them:

> The bird in a cage is in need of promenade
>
> The sleepwalker is in need of anemic sunshine (*Bei Dao* 178)

Bei Dao does not elaborate on the relationship between the bird and the sleepwalker in this example from "Daydream." Just as Yaoliang Song maintains, poets of the *Today* school "shear off direct expressions and pursue instead anfractuous and contrapuntal presentations" (61).

This distance between the phrases and their referents gives his poetry "an abstract, anonymous, and universal frame" as Bonnie S. McDougall suggests, and leads to multiple interpretations of a poem (228). Just as Bei Dao maintains that "a writer must have complex positions and perspectives," "Daydream" leaves open space for the reader's imagination to conjure up a story between images that are mostly drawn from nature in his "true to life" "artistry" (*Gulao* 151; Chien Chang, *Qing* 266). Bei Dao maintains that this obscurity is indispensable because "a direct confrontation in the ideological dimension renders literature an echo of official discourse" (*Shijian* 255).

The Self-Image and Ars Poetica*:*

Intensity, Transcendence, and Animosity

As Fang-xi Liu suggests, "Misty poetry is a return to 'people's literature,'" and in Bei Dao's idiosyncratic view, a poet must confront the dark side of the human condition including "pain," "suffering," and "the absurdity of existence" (Fang-xi Liu 313; Bei Dao, "Secrecy" 231). Though some critics, such as Simon Patton, maintain that Bei Dao writes in two styles, one along a vein of "protest poems," and the other of a lyric strain, Bei Dao declares that poetry always conveys the intensity of feelings: "poetry must have passion and imagination as well as inexplicable power and things that make one dizzy" (Patton 139; Bei Dao, *Shibai* 285). For example, in tone, "Daydream" is passionately articulated in an oratory voice delivered in lines liberally accentuated with stresses. Moreover, for this very reason, tragedies and war are apposite materials for poetry: poetry that served as "my reference is [poetry of] the first half of the twentieth century. . . . War, valediction, and pain at that time supply profuse afflatus for the poetry. To me, poetry is an art of suffering," writes Bei Dao (*Shibai* 288). His poem "The Answer" deftly illustrates this viewpoint: "then let all the bitter water instill into my heart . . . ; / then let humankind select again the peak of existence" (*Rose* 6).

On the relationship between poetry and the world, Bei Dao maintains that while poetry is enmeshed in the world, poetry also transcends it:

> Poetry certainly is concerned with many dimensions including politics, but poetry also transcends

politics. . . . Transcending the limits of civilization, culture, religion, and language, poetry embodies imagination and creativity outside the borders. (qtd. in Ruan 38)

Bei Dao maintains that realism is not the telos of his work: "I'm always trying to write what's beyond reality, rather than reality itself" ("Reality").

Moreover, the idea of animosity is in accordance with Bei Dao's *ars poetica* calling for an ever-vigilant skepticism against stagnation in both poetry and the significance of the mainstream. A poet should take a critical and oppositional stance toward his own poetry, "an 'animosity' a writer has for himself," suggests Bei Dao (*Gulao* 153). The concept of animosity also explains the tense relationship between a writer and his time. . . . A writer should distance himself from the mainstream and take a skeptical and critical stance toward all power and its discourses. (*Gulao* 151)

"Poetry must retain its small-audience consciousness," maintains Bei Dao (qtd. in Wai Tong Liu 74). In concert with Bei Dao's idea of animosity is the belletristic concept of "pure literature" among dissident writers including Bei Dao: for them, "the most important thing is to keep one's distance from power" ("Secrecy" 239-40).

This belief in dissonance explains the skepticism permeating his poetry, and Bei Dao suggests that this skeptical lens is a product of his time: "we live in a time . . . that calls for persistent queries and skepticalness," he says (*Gulao* 153). A fine example of this skepticism is his preference for the idea of paradox, which exemplifies an attitude welcoming volatileness and multiple interpretations (Dian Li 115, 128). To foreground the excruciating irrationality of the Cultural Revolution and the absurdity of life in general, Bei Dao is fond of the use of paradox forged frequently out of "split imagery," Dian Li's term, which Dian Li defines as "a compound image in which antithetical elements function to produce responses of ambiguity and paradox" (128). Another critical view maintains that "a fusion of various modernist styles," such as the paradox Dian Li suggests, is found in Bei Dao's poetry ("Chinese Literature"). Bei Dao's adoption of Western styles attests to the interrelatedness of literature. Bei Dao's idea of globalization exemplifies the interrelatedness of literature. The next section will discuss Bei Dao's idea of this interrelatedness of literature.

Globalization and Literature's Interrelatedness

Bei Dao's idea of globalization exemplifies the interrelatedness of literature in our time of globalization. A poet with a global stature, Bei Dao interprets globalization as a reality with two facets people now share: "one is the globalization of power and capital that is carving up the world; the other is the globalization of the seeds of language and the spirit that are settling on fertile ground wherever the storm may take them" (Bei Dao, "Out" 22). On the current state of affairs of globalization, Bei

Dao suggests in 2015 that "global power and capital continue to divide and rule the world" (Foreword).

For Bei Dao, *Today* realizes the second sort of globalization, bearing upon

> the oppression of and resistance to institutional discourse, the globalizing conspiracy of power and capital, the spirit of 'China as youth' set against the backdrop of grim reality, and the experience of growing up and the dreams of a generation. (*Gulao* 182)

In a speech delivered in 2015, Bei Dao suggests that *Today* "fights against . . . not only totalitarianism but also . . . the mediocracy of aestheticism and life's triviality" ("Zai"). The inclusivity and the globalization of poetry since the twentieth century are, in Bei Dao's view, suggested by his term of "international poetry" that "crosses the borders of the nation-state, race, and language to gain unprecedented international vision and corresponding international influence" (*Shijian* 323). Another remark points to the structures at work in this globalization: On the occasion of "the third Princeton Biennial Poetry Festival" held in 2013 to which both Graham and Bei Dao were invited, Paul Muldoon observed: "You now have poetry festivals all over the world, pulling in really great people from all over" to discuss and share poetry (Timpane). Literature and people are interrelated in the globally extended space. The next section suggests that the universal subjectivity Bei Dao's poem "Daydream" advances is an excellent solution to meliorate the self-other relationship in intimate global interrelatedness.

Bei Dao's "Daydream" and Fichte's Universal Subjectivity

Composed in 1986, the long poem "Daydream" cited by Graham in her poem "Event Horizon" is a work of Bei Dao's pre-exile period before an expatriate life away from China from the year 1989 to 2007 (Bei Dao, *Shibai* 296 and *Gulao* 165). In addition to the space between images he intentionally leaves, at its closing, the poem intimates an ethic of a high awareness of others as subjects, advancing a universal subjectivity, in my analysis, as an apt solution to ameliorate the self-other relationship in this age of intimate global connectivity. The poem also examines, in terms of historiography, how one may confront the aftermath of a crisis. "Daydream" ruminates over and panegyrizes the value of dreams and love in the wake of the departure of a loved one.

In "Daydream," the departure of the beloved is compared to one's relationship with history, as both are irrevocable, prior to the moment in which the narrator speaks, and subject to interpretation. Guang-ming Bi suggests that "the main concern" of "Daydream" is the feelings of loss of a person's contemporaries (161). Si-ping Yang suggests that "Daydream" is expanded from Bei Dao's early poem "Resume" and is "a national allegory and cultural imagination of the growing-up history of a generation" (29). Another source of "Daydream" could be found in an earlier love poem entitled "Comet," which also possesses a theme of departure (*Rose* 32). Though the departure is given in the form of a statement, it poses as a question for the narrator, and this riddle is unsolved at the poem's closing:

> The white crane unfurls a piece of fluttering paper
> on which is written your answer
> that I know nothing about.
>
> You did not return as scheduled. (*Bei Dao* 195)

Family life in his youth accounts for this pervasive theme of difficulty in communication in his poetry: Bei Dao's poetry reflects on a "traditional Chinese father [who] put a lot of pressure on" him ("Secrecy" 228); he also notes that ever since he was "a teenager," he has "had difficulties communicating" and started to compose poems as "a way of communicating" ("Secrecy" 227-28).

The narrator's effort to explain the loved one's departure produces a wry intrigue in this poem, a "tragedy" about lost love and the turbulent nature of the time (*Bei Dao* 194). About dreams and love at a time of crisis and loss, "Daydream" recounts a series of dismal episodes, including the loved one's egress, the lacuna of space and dialogue, the speaker's symbolic death, war, and a funeral, set in a bleak landscape. The speaker of this poem bemoans a lost love in an almost incantatory refrain— "You did not return as scheduled"—resonating throughout the poem (*Bei Dao* 173, 176, 187, 195).

One problem in the epoch of loss and war depicted in the poem is the lack of dissension ("no seeds of animosity")

(*Bei Dao* 174). The young generation needs dialogue and space, yet this wish is unfulfilled and denied by capital and power:

> In a small shop,
>
> a money bill, a razor blade
>
> and an extremely venomous pesticide
>
> was born. (*Bei Dao* 178)

This denial has several consequences including the narrator's symbolic premature death and a newspaper that has concealed its "passion" about journalism (*Bei Dao* 179).

Next, the speaker suggests that once people are interpreted by history, they are historicized and enter history:

This is an empty museum.

Whoever within it

is presumed to be an item of display. (*Bei Dao* 180)

Then the dead of war announce to the living their historical

position related to wars in the past:

You are not survivors.

You will never find homes. (*Bei Dao* 185)

However, "new concepts" of this epoch contradict this declaration, and the speaker suggests that desire may reinvigorate the Chinese language that has become "stale" (*Bei Dao* 185, 195, 186). The magazine *Today* Bei Dao cofounded is one of the publications in a literary movement to revive the language: "The momentum of a widespread movement of new literature in the 1980s is avant-garde literature" whose wellspring is "the underground writings from the late 1960s to the 1970s that finally were publically published and read" ("Zai"). In reality, "*Jintian (Today)* was the second magazine" to be posted "on the wall" in 1978 during the Democracy Wall movement in Beijing, and Bei Dao's poem "The Answer" "was reproduced on countless wall posters" that year (La Piana; Weinberger 114).

On a "winter day," the "lone" speaker sets out in a quest for "passion," yet finds "no dreams" while examining the tradition of the Chinese empire symbolized by the Forbidden City ("a city within a city") (*Bei Dao* 188-90, 193). As the poem's title suggests, daydreaming through one's imagination is better than dreamlessness, having no visions to change the status quo. The title of the poem befits Bei Dao's habits of composition ever since he started writing poetry in 1968:

> After work, I often wandered about . . . and some detached chaotic threads of thought suddenly formed into sentences. . . . When I write I am often in a kind of sleeplike condition, a false sleep which gets my imagination started. ("Secrecy" 229, 236)

Pessimism ("a death report") permeates the present moment, yet a flicker of hope is revived at the sight of "twilight" toward the poem's open ending when the narrator cannot comprehend the departed person's "answer" (*Bei Dao* 194-95). Bei Dao's view on the mission of poetry explains the hope in this closing: "poets . . . let everything wonderful enter people's hearts deeply" ("Wo" 90). The light of hope, such as the twilight in "Daydream," is in my view what distinguishes Bei Dao as a global figure from innumerable others. Credited with the prowess to augur change in duress and adversity, his poetry, when recalled, is like gold dust bestrewing from a beacon-like mind.

Like "Event Horizon," in a keen awareness of others, "Daydream" ends with the epiphany pertaining to the respect, in an equal subject position, toward others and their ideas (*Bei Dao* 195). The ending illustrates a self-other relationship defined by Fichte as a relationship between free and rational beings, giving due respect for the subjectivity of oneself and others. Fichte maintains that every individual has "reason and freedom," and the fact is recognized first by oneself: "*A finite rational being cannot posit itself without ascribing a free efficacy to itself*"

(Fichte 43, 18; Williams 136-37). This freedom stems from one's subjectivity: "*Activity that reverts into itself in general* (I-hood, subjectivity) *is the mark of a rational being*" (Fichte 18). Next, Fichte suggests that one must also ascribe "such efficacy to others," recognizing their subjectivity (29). Fichte founds this concept of an individual on the interpersonal relationship and defines a person as one in the human species (37-38). Therefore, Fichte maintains that a person treats another person as a rational being having freedom in subjectivity in "a relation between rational beings," what he calls "a relation of right," by recognizing each other as "*a free being*" and "*limit[ing] my freedom through the concept of the possibility of his freedom*" (51, 39, 49). In other words, on the self-other relationship, the ending of "Daydream" affirms Fichte's concept of universal subjectivity, which fosters a libertarian and egalitarian self-other relationship for our age of a heightened sense of others in global interconnectedness.

Conclusion: The Globally Extended Space and the Interrelatedness of Literature

To Bei Dao, the globally extended space is deterritorializing. Bei Dao's disinclination toward the obstructing of social progress and his deep-seated belief in freedom and human dignity spread from China to the global arena. In 1993 Bei Dao was banned from entering China because in 1989 he started a letter calling for the Chinese government to free prisoners of conscience

(Janssen 261; Zhao 137; La Piana; Bei Dao, "Out" 22). In 2009, Bei Dao was one among those who signed a letter requesting the government of Iran release the Canadian Iranian journalist and director Maziar Bahari ("Editorial"). At the same time, owing to our interrelatedness, locally rooted literature with global attributes and validity can become global. Though he is not Macedonian, Swedish, Korean, German, or Moroccan, Bei Dao won the Golden Wreath Award from the former Yugoslav Republic of Macedonia in 2015 in addition to the Cikada Prize and the PEN Tucholsky Prize from Sweden in 2014 and 1990, the first Changwon KC International Literary Prize for Poetry from Korea, the Jeanette Schocken Literary Prize from Germany in 2005, and the International Poetry Argana Award from Morocco in 2002 ("Struga"; "Professor"; "Bei

Dao (1949-)"; "An Evening").

Chapter 7

Conclusion

My Theories and Argument

In this book I examine the fallout in theories, culture, and literature after the extension of space in globalization. The stretching of space beyond a nation-state's borders is a crucial mainstay of the intensified and accelerating interconnectedness and interdependency among govern-ments, economies, and people. To a plethora of scholars in global studies, interconnectedness and interdependency are two of the signature outcomes of globalization. Moreover, to me and to a great number of globalization scholars including Castells, Ferguson, Mansbach, and Saskia Sassen, Information and Communication Technologies (ICT) and transportation technology are the material conditions of the extending of space, and neoliberalism conduces to the global extension of space (Ferguson and Mansbach 114). An extension of space in this age of globalization ensues where the territorial space of the nation-state connects with global space, defined as real or virtual space among more than two peoples, cultures, or the globe's geographical regions. This extension also subserves as a defining characteristic of the era's spatial interconnectedness. Communication and transportation technology realizes and accelerates this correlating of national and global space. Capitalist motives founded on receiving more revenue generated from tourism and air transportation opened the doors between hostile countries including those between China and Taiwan.

I maintain in two theoretical chapters, Chapter 2 and Chapter 3, of this book that space and human rights, including freedom, are global-local in multiple dimensions and are deterritorializing. In Chapters 4 to 6 on poetry and poetics I argue that modern and contemporary Taiwanese and American poetry probes the extension's effects on freedom, the human mind, locality, and poetics. I examine the oeuvres of five Taiwanese poets—Chou-yu Cheng, Wan-yu Lin, Hsiung Hung, Hsia Yu, and Yin Ling—and two American poets Graham and Bei Dao on the globally extended space in globalization. Their works eulogize freedom or register its metamorphosis. Their poems scrutinize the extension's impacts on the mind including the deepening of loneliness, the dominance of the unconscious during global travel, and nostalgia for the territories, heritages, and space of childhood. And their works also portray global interconnectedness and its implications in poetics such as interrelatedness and openness.

Chapter 1 introduces this book's two parts on theories and poetry, respectively, and my argument, theories, and terms on space and on human rights, including freedom, in the globally extended space in this book's seven chapters. I suggest in Chapter 2 that in current theories space is multiscalar, deterritorialized, and multi-dimensional. In Chapter 2 I construct my three dimensions of space including the haecceitic dimension, social dimension, and social and international dimension, and two secondary dimensions including the affective secondary dimension within the social dimension and virtual secondary dimension in the social and international dimension. I also establish descriptors for all three of my dimensions including two descriptors of the haecceitic dimension—heterogeneity in constitution and deterritorialization. My descriptor for the social dimension is relatedness, while my descriptor for the social and international dimension is interrelatedness in globalization.

Moreover, Chapter 2 suggests that recent theories on people in space explore mostly the haecceitic dimension of space and the heterogeneity and deterritorialization of space. I maintain as well that recent literary theories on space theorize space as ontological, cultural, and deterritorialized. Globalization in recent scholarship is defined as changes and as its dimensions. I suggest that recent scholarly unanimity defines globalization as its two impacts and dimensions, interrelatedness and interdependency.

Chapter 3 contextualizes my theory within current theories on space and human rights such as freedom. Scholars suggest that freedom has an argosy of discrepant definitions because freedom is not just an ethical value but also a moral, legal, and political value (Frost 75-77; Moyn, *The Last* 226-27). I suggest in my own theory on the globally extended space and freedom in Chapter 3 that freedom is ensured or reconceptualized in the globally extended space, and in some situations, more by global politics and transnational and global institutions or groups than by domestic institutions and organizations or the nation-states. Human rights are local values in a nation and global values in global civil society because, in the three dimensions I posit, human rights are abstract values, national values, and international and global values. Human rights have their detractors and supporters in ideologies, among people, and in movements. I suggest in Chapter 3 that human rights are not adverse to nationalism in the nation-state, or to isolationism globally. Some people oppose the practice of human rights because in the globally extended space human rights flow with fewer obstructions than politics and people as both Castells and Bauman maintain (Bauman, "Media" 301). Anti-globalization movements and ideologies, however, can remain neutral to human rights, protect human rights, or violate human rights as I observe. Finally, Chapter 3 suggests that globalization is an intersectional and inclusive field and approach for incalculable scholars across disciplines.

In Part II, I argue that Taiwanese and American poetry on the globally extended space fathoms the aftereffects of the extension of space, for example, the ensuring of freedom and the reconceptualization of freedom. Other impacts of the extension include the intensification of loneliness by swindles and commercialization, the alleviation of solitude by global travel, the surfacing of the unconscious and the recollection of space of childhood during global travel, and nostalgia for territories and heritages. Still other outcomes of the extension of space encompass dread of war and global politics, global interconnectivity among strangers, and global interrelatedness. In my discussion of Taiwanese and American poetry on the globally extended space in Chapter 4 and Chapter 5, respectively, I coined

267

my own literary terms including "poetics of inter-relatedness and openness" on interrelatedness and the strategies of indeterminacy and experimentality in poetry, "poetics of interrelatedness" defined as the interrelated self in poetry, "prodigal place" on a place loaded with other loci and times, and the "othering of place" about the absent other's presence.

In Chapter 4 on Taiwanese poetry on the globally extended space published after the 1950s, I maintain that in his poetry Chou-yu Cheng honors freedom, suggests the inviolability of national borders and the global defense of national security, and construes nostalgia as longing for national territories and heritages. Wan-yu Lin gives her insights on loneliness intensified by fraudulent schemes and by the commercialization of the relationships among people. Wan-yu Lin's poetry also elucidates the power of global travel in countering this solitude. The poem "Writing a Poem in Jet Lag" written by Hsiung Hung portrays the globetrotter's jet lag and space lag and illuminates nostalgia as the craving for space of childhood. Hsia Yu in her book of poems *First Person* renders the global interconnectedness among strangers in a poetics of interrelatedness and openness in my coined term. Yin Ling's poem "A White Dove Flew Over" suggests that freedom in the globally extended space is defined more by global politics than by a nation-state and chronicles fear about wars and global politics in the globally extended space. Chapter 5 and Chapter 6 compare the poetry written by American poets Graham and Bei Dao. I argue that in a poetics of interrelatedness, American poet Graham imagines a self interrelated with other people in her poetry. I maintain in Chapter 6 that Bei Dao's idea of globalization affirms literature's global interrelatedness. Moreover, Bei Dao's poem "Daydream" illuminates a universal subjectivity in Fichte's theory. In the next section, I will examine the problematics in the globally extended space Chou-yu Cheng's poetry already intimates.

Closed Space in the Globally Extended Space?

The globally extended space does not include all nation-states' territories and cannot always prevail over nation-states' power within national territories as Chou-yu Cheng's poem "Border Inn" suggests. Yet national territories can be located within the globally extended space. There is closed space in the globally extended space to this effect. The policies and laws of political entities, the national dimension of human rights, nationalism, religions, cultures, customs, and communities have owned and may retain closed space in the globally extended space. What if the space in certain cities, nation-states, or regions is closed? This is a topic for scholars' research in the future.

The Globally Extended
Space, Rights, and Literature

On both theories and poetry, my book affirms the mostly auspicious direction of the positive developments of the extension of space and the ineluctable global facets of space, human rights, emotions, people, the nation-state, and poetry. As the book does with the dimensions and descriptors of space, theories on space and freedom, literary terms, and readings of poetry, other scholarly endeavors could help clarify the global-cum-local reality and literature of this era. However, a consensus about the definitions of human rights has not been reached by all nation-states and cultures. The book looks to future missions to reform customs and formulate standards of human rights.

Notes

Chapter 4

[1] I gained this information from the staff at National Quemoy University over the phone.

[2] Unless otherwise indicated, all translations from Chinese sources are my own.

[3] Unless otherwise noted, all of the biographical information about Wan-yu Lin is from Wan-yu Lin's e-mail message in Chinese to the author on May 20, 2019 and from Wan-yu Lin's other e-mail messages to the author in 2019.

[4] Except the postscript written in Chinese, the poetry in English quoted from *First Person* is Bradbury's translation.

Chapter 6

[1] Unless otherwise noted, all translations are my own.

Works Cited

"107 xueniandu di 2 xueqi tongshi kechengbiao." *Center for General Education*, 15 Feb. 2019, www.cge.ntnu.edu.tw/uploads/student/tw/6.pdf.

Agnew, John A. *Place and Politics: The Geographical Mediation of State and Society*. Routledge, 2015.

"The American Poets Prizes." *American Poet*, vol. 53, Fall/Winter 2017, pp. 10-14. *EBSCOhost*, search.ebscohost.com/login.aspx?direct=true&db=hlh&AN=127910000&lang=zh-tw&site=ehost-live.

"An Evening with Bei Dao." *Words without Borders*, 1 Mar. 2012, www.wordswithoutborders.org/events/an-evening-with-bei-dao. Accessed 12 Oct. 2016.

Andersen, Hans. *Fairy Tales from Hans Andersen*. T. C. & E. C. Jack, 1908.

Ang, Ien. "Beyond Chinese Groupism: Chinese Australians between Assimilation, Multiculturalism and Diaspora." *Belonging to the Nation: General Change, Identity and the Chinese Diaspora*, edited by Edmund Terence Gomez and Gregor Benton. Routledge, 2015, pp. 27-39.

Ashford, Elizabeth. "The Nature of Violations of the Human Right to Subsistence." *Human Rights: Moral or Political?*, edited by Adam Etinson, Oxford UP, 2018, pp. 337-62.

Atwood, William G. *Fryderyk Chopin: Pianist from Warsaw.* Columbia UP, 1987.

Bachelard, Gaston. *The Poetics of Space: The Classic Look at How We Experience Intimate Places.* Translated by Maria Jolas, Orion, 1964.

Bai Ling. "Qizai shi shang de hudie—xu Yin Ling shiji *Yizhi baige feiguo*." *A White Dove Passing by.* By Yin Ling. Chiu Ko, 1997, pp. 9-25.

---. "The Traveller and Chivalrous Person: The Spirit of Chivalrous Traveller and the Inflection of Time and Space in Zheng Chou-Yu's Poetry." *MingDao Journal of General Education*, vol. 2, 2007, pp. 107-48.

Bauman, Zygmunt. "Liquid Fear." *The New Bauman*

Reader: Thinking Sociologically in Liquid Modern Times, edited by Tony Blackshaw, Manchester UP, 2016, pp. 346-63.

---. "'Liquid Modernity' Fifteen Years after (2015)." *The New Bauman Reader: Thinking Sociologically in Liquid Modern Times*, edited by Tony Blackshaw, Manchester UP, 2016, pp. 391-402.

---. "Media." *The New Bauman Reader: Thinking Sociologically in Liquid Modern Times*, edited by Tony Blackshaw, Manchester UP, 2016, pp. 282-303.

Beck, Ulrich, and Elisabeth Beck-Gernsheim. *Distance Love: Personal Life in the Global Age*. Translated by Rodney Livingstone, Polity, 2014.

Bei Dao. *Bei Dao shixuan* [*Selected Poetry of Bei Dao*]. 2nd ed., Xin shiji, 1987.

---. Foreword. *Poetry and Conflict Anthology*, edited by Bei Dao, et al., Chinese UP, 2015. *Project MUSE*, muse.jhu.edu.

---. *Gulao de diyi* [*Ancient Animosity*]. Oxford UP, 2012.

---. "A Note from the Editor." *Words & the World*, edited by Gilbert C. F. Fong, Shelby K. Y. Chan, Lucas Klein, Amy Ho Kit Yin, and Bei Dao, Chinese UP, 2011, p. 13.

---. "Out of the Cradle, Endlessly Sleepwalking." *World Literature Today*, vol. 82, no. 6, Nov.-Dec. 2008, pp. 20-22.

---. *The Rose of Time: New and Selected Poems*. Translated by Yanbing Chen, David Hinton, Maiping Chen, Iona Man-Cheong, Bonnie S. McDougall, and Eliot Weinberger, edited by Eliot Weinberger, New Directions, 2010.

---. "Secrecy and Truth." Interview by Anne Wedell-Wedellsborg. *Cultural Encounters: China, Japan, and the West: Essays Commemorating 25 Years of East Asian Studies at the University of Aarhus*, edited by Søren Clausen, Roy Starrs, and Anne Wedell-Wedellsborg, Aarhus UP, 1995, pp. 227-40.

---. *Shibai zhi shu* [*The Book of Failure*]. Shantou UP, 2004.

---. *Shijian de meigui*. Zhongguo wenshi, 2005.

---. "Wo men meitian de taiyang." *Shanghai Literature*, vol. 5, 1981, pp. 90-91. *CNKI*, www.cnki.net.

---. "Zai tianya: Bei Dao, Hu Sang shiji jiangtan" ["At the Sky's Edge: A Dialogue between Bei Dao and Hu Sang"]. 23 Oct. 2015, Department of Sinophone Literatures, National Dong Hwa U, Hualien, Taiwan. MP3 file.

"Bei Dao (1949-)." *Cikada-Priset/The Cikada Prize*, 2014, www.cikada-priset.se/. Accessed 12 Oct. 2016.

Benhabib, Seyla. "Democratic Sovereignty and Trans-national Law: On Legal Utopianism and Democratic Skepticism." *Critical Theory in Critical Times: Transforming the Global Political and Economic Order*, edited by Penelope Deutscher and Cristina Lafont, Columbia UP, 2017, pp. 21-46.

Bi, Guang-ming. *History and Life*. Showwe, 2016.

Bob, Clifford. "Globalization and the Social Construction of Human Rights Campaigns." *Globalization and*

Human Rights, edited by Alison Brysk, U of California P, 2002, pp. 133-47.

Bowen, John. *The Economic Geography of Air Transportation: Space, Time, and the Freedom of the Sky*. Routledge, 2010.

Broadcasting Corporation of China. "Zhuanfang shiren Cheng Chou-yu." *National Central Library*, 11 Jun. 1985, *Digital Audio Visual Archive System*, dava.ncl.edu.tw/MetadataInfo.aspx?funtype=0&id= 391774.

Burt, Stephen. "American Poetry at the End of Millennium." *The Cambridge History of American Poetry*, edited by Alfred Bendixen and Stephen Burt. Cambridge UP, 2015, pp. 1144-66.

Campbell, David. *National Deconstruction: Violence, Identity, and Justice in Bosnia*. U of Minnesota P, 1998.

Castells, Manuel. *End of Millennium*. 2nd ed., Wiley-Blackwell, 2010.

---. *The Rise of the Network Society*. 2nd ed., Wiley-Blackwell, 2010.

Castree, Noel. "Place: Connections and Boundaries in an Interdependent World." *Key Concepts in Geography*, edited by Nicholas J. Clifford, Sarah L. Holloway, Stephen P. Rice, and Gill Valentine, 2nd ed., Sage, 2009, pp. 153-72.

Chang, Chien. *Qing yu yun: Liangan xiandai shi jijin.* Niang chu ban, 2011.

---. "Zheng Chouyu qingshi shier shi." *Huigu liangan 50 nian wenxue xueshu yantaohui lunwenji*, edited by Department of Chinese Literature, Chinese Culture University, vol. 1, Chinese Culture University, 2004, pp. 3-23.

Chang, Mei-Fang. "The Objects and Skills of Cheng Chou-yu's Language of Poetry." *Contemporary Poetics*, vol. 2, 2006, pp. 63-80.

Chang Mo, editor. *Xiandai nü shiren xuanji, 1952-2011* [*Modern Women Poets, 1952-2011*]. 1st ed., Elite,

2011.

Chen, Fang-ming. *Mei yu xunmei*. Linking, 2015.

Chen, I-chih. *Fengge de dansheng: xiandai shiren zhuanti lungao*. Asian Culture, 2017.

Chen, Jing-Yi. "Between Bay Leaf and Bodhi—the Poetry Steering and Life Course of Xiong-Hong." *Journal of Chien Hsin University*, vol. 36, no. 1, 2016, pp. 59-75.

Chen, Tsun-shing, director. *The Inspired Island: Port of Mists*. Fisfisa Media, 2012, disc 1.

Chen, Wen-Chen. "Self-Writing in Yin-Ling's Poems—Using *A Pigeon Flying by* as the Subject for Discussion." *Bulletin of Taiwanese Poetics*, vol. 27, 2016, pp. 47-67.

Chen, Yongguo. "Becoming-Obscure: A Constant in the Development of Modern Chinese Poetry." *Modern Language Quarterly*, vol. 69, no.1, Mar. 2008, pp. 81-96.

Chen, Zhong-Yi. "The 'Axis' Tension of Modern Poetry

Language." *Taiwan Poetry*, vol. 22, 2013, pp. 7-31.

Cheng, Chou-yu. "Caixiang liming de yanse." *Unitas*, vol. 18, no. 8, 2002, pp. 12-17.

---. *Cheng Chou-yu shi xuanji.* 1974. Zhiwen, 2010.

---. "Cong qingqing zijin dao jiangwan Zheng Chouyu." *YouTube*, 15 Jun. 2017, www.youtube.com/watch?v=qAVu4h8VRmo&feature=youtu.beyoutu.be/qAVu4h8VRmo.

---. *Jimo de ren zuozhe kanhua.* Hung-Fan, 1993.

---. "Se (2)—qing, shi juli de secai." *Unitas*, vol. 18, no. 12, 2002, pp. 24-27.

---. *Yanrenxing.* Hung-Fan, 1980.

---. "Yong shi wei huaxia wenming pi bazi: jie zi de mei, du shi de yun." *Zai renwen lushang yujian shengming daoshi: gei weilai yisheng de shitang ke*, Global Views-Commonwealth, 2017, pp. 10-35.

---. *Zheng Chouyu shiji I: 1951-1968.* Hung-Fan, 2003.

Cheng, Guang-wei. *Zhongguo dangdai shigeshi [A History of Contemporary Chinese Poetry].* Renmin U of China P, 2003.

"Chinese Literature." *Columbia Electronic Encyclopedia,* 6th ed., 2016, Q2.

"Chronology." *The Cambridge Companion to Chopin,* edited by Jim Samson, Cambridge UP, 1992, pp. vii-xi.

"Chubanren wei Cheng Chou-yu xunzong." *Heping de yibo: bainian shige wanzai chengping,* Chou Ta-Kuan Cultural and Educational Foundation, 2011, pp. 384-90.

Chung, Emily. *Lin Wan-yu jiqi xinshi yanjiu.* 2015. National Changhua U of Education, MA thesis.

Chung, Ling. "Wushi niandai qingyue de nü gaoyin—Hsiung Hung." *Taiwan xiandangdai zuojia yanjiu ziliao huibian,* vol. 98, Taiwan National Museum of Taiwan Literature, 2017, pp. 157-68.

Clark, Benjamin. Review of *Salsa. Chinese Literature Today,* vol. 5, no. 2, pp. 98-99.

Cochrane, Feargal. *Migration and Security in the Global*

Age: Diaspora Communities and Conflict. Routledge, 2015.

Cohen, Robin, and Olivia Sheringham. *Encountering Difference: Diasporic Traces, Creolizing Spaces.* Polity, 2016.

Cuowu (ci Cheng Chou-yu, qu, yanchang Li Taixiang) Cheng Chou-yu qinzi langsong bing jiangjie ziji de chengming zhi zuo. video.iphone.gb.net/mp3/%E8 %A9%A9%E4%BA%BA%E9%84%AD%E6%84% 81%E4%BA%88%E8%88%8A%E9%87%91%E5 %B1%B1%E5%B7%9E%E7%AB%8B%E5%A4% A7%E5%AD%B8%E8%AC%9B%E5%BA%A7- zheng-chouyu-11913-video-2.html.

"Czech Demonstrators Surround a Soviet [. . .]." *Times, The (United Kingdom)*, 20 Aug. 2011, p. 79. *EBSCOhost*, search.ebscohost.com/login.aspx?direct =true&db=nfh&AN=7EH50806010&lang=zh-tw& site=ehost-live.

Damrosch, David. *What Is World Literature?* Princeton UP,

2003.

Darian-Smith, Eve, and Philip C. McCarty. *The Global Turn: Theories, Research Designs, and Methods for Global Studies.* U of California P, 2017.

Deleuze, Gilles, and Félix Guattari. *A Thousand Plateaus: Capitalism and Schizophrenia.* Translated by Brian Massumi, U of Minnesota P, 1987.

Department of Household Registration Affairs, MOI. "02-03 Population by Marital Status." *Department of Statistics*, 20 Apr. 2019, www.moi.gov.tw/stat/node. aspx?Z=1&sn=6826.

Du Ye. *Xinshi xin tansuo.* Showwe, 2016.

"Editorial." *Index on Censorship*, vol. 38, no. 3, 2009, pp. 6-7. *Academic Search Premier*, web.b.ebscohost. com/ehost.

Ehlers, Sarah. "Jorie Graham's Passion for the Reel: The Lyric Subject Encounters the Image." *Mosaic*, vol. 50, no. 2, 2017, pp. 29–46.

"Event Horizon." *Collins Dictionary of Astronomy*, edited

by John Daintith and William Gould, Collins, 2006. *Credo Reference*, search.credoreference.com.

Faulconbridge, James R., and Jonathan V. Beaverstock. "Globalization: Interconnected Worlds." *Key Concepts in Geography*, edited by Nicholas J. Clifford, Sarah L. Holloway, Stephen P. Rice, and Gill Valentine, 2nd ed., Sage, 2009, pp. 331-43.

Feng, Congde. *A Tiananmen Journal*. 1st ed., Ziyou wenhua, 2009.

Ferguson, Yale H., and Richard W. Mansbach. *Globalization: The Return of Borders to a Borderless World?* Routledge, 2012.

Fichte, Johann Gottlieb. *Foundations of Natural Right*. Translated by Michael Baur, edited by Frederick Neuhouser, Cambridge UP, 2000.

"Forward Prizes 2016." *Forward Arts Foundation*, 2016, www.forwardartsfoundation.org/forward-prizes-for-poetry/about/. Accessed 9 Oct. 2016.

Frost, Rainer. "A Critical Theory of Human Rights—Some

Groundwork." *Critical Theory in Critical Times: Transforming the Global Political and Economic Order*, edited by Penelope Deutscher and Cristina Lafont, Columbia UP, 2017, pp. 74-88.

García Canclini, Néstor. *Imagined Globalization*, translated by George Yúdice, Duke UP, 2014.

Gardner, Thomas. "From 'Jorie Graham's Incandescence.'" *Jorie Graham: Essays on the Poetry*, edited by Thomas Gardner, U of Wisconsin P, 2005, pp. 113-46.

Giddens, Anthony. *The Consequences of Modernity*. Stanford UP, 1990.

---. *Europe in the Global Age*. Polity, 2007.

---. *Modernity and Self-Identity: Self and Society in the Late Modern Age*. Stanford UP, 1991.

Giles, Paul. "Transnationalism and Classic American Literature." *PMLA*, vol. 118, no. 1, Jan. 2003, pp. 62-77. *EBSCOhost*, 0-search.ebscohost.com.opac.lib. ntnu.edu.tw/login.aspx?direct=true&db=mzh&AN= 2003530004&lang=zh-tw&site=eds-live.

Golan, Galia. *Reform Rule in Czechoslovakia: The Dubček Era 1968-1969*. Cambridge UP, 1973.

Graham, Jorie. "America's Understanding of the Planet." *The Big Think, Inc.*, 3 Apr. 2008, bigthink.com/ videos/americas-understanding-of-the-planet. Accessed 9 Oct. 2016.

---. *"How Has the Internet Changed Language?" The Big Think, Inc.*, 3 Apr. 2008, bigthink.com/videos/how-has-the-internet-changed-language. Accessed 9 Oct. 2016.

---. "Later in Life." *The Big Think, Inc.*, 3 Apr. 2008, bigthink.com/videos/jorie-graham-reads-later-in-life. Accessed 9 Oct. 2016.

---. *Materialism*. Ecco, 1993.

---. "My Skin Is." *London Review of Books*, vol. 40, issue 13, 5 Jul. 2018, p. 22.

---. *Overlord: Poems*. 1st ed., HarperCollins, 2005.

---. *Sea Change: Poems*. 1st ed., Ecco, 2009.

---. "Something of Moment." *Ploughshares*, vol. 27, issue

4, Winter 2001-02, pp. 7-9.

---. *Swarm.* 1st ed., Ecco, 2000.

Gürüz, Kemal. *Higher Education and International Student Mobility in the Global Knowledge Economy.* State U of New York P, 2008.

Ha, Kim-lan. "Suming wanggu? Jiegou dianfu?—shixi Yin Ling shuxie." *Bulletin of Taiwanese Poetics*, vol. 10, 2007, pp. 279-303.

"Ha Kim-lan." *Department of Chinese Literature, Tamkang University*, 20 Jul. 2019, www.tacx.tku. edu.tw/info/index.php?PID=14.

Hall, Peter A., Wade Jacoby, Jonah Levy, and Sophie Meunier. Introduction: The Politics of Representation in the Global Age. *The Politics of Representation in the Global Age: Identification, Mobilization, and Adjudication,* edited by Peter A. Hall, Wade Jacoby, Jonah Levy, and Sophie Meunier, Cambridge UP, 2014, pp. 1-25.

Hall, Stuart. "The Local and the Global: Globalization and

Ethnicity." *Dangerous Liaisons: Gender, Nation, and Postcolonial Perspectives*, edited by Anne McCintock, Aamir Mufti, and Ella Shohat, U of Minnesota P, 1997, pp. 173-87.

Harsch, Michael F. *The Power of Dependence: NATO-UN Cooperation in Crisis Management*. 1st ed., Oxford UP, 2015. *Oxford Scholarship Online*, www. oxfordscholarship.com/view/10.1093/acprof:oso/97 80198722311.001.0001/acprof-9780198722311.

Harvey, David. *Cosmopolitanism and the Geographies of Freedom*. Columbia UP, 2009.

Hevesi, Dennis, and Daniel E. Slotnik. "Curtis Bill Pepper, Reporter and Traveler, Is Dead at 96." *New York Times*, 5 Apr. 2014, A19. *EBSCO*, search.ebscohost. com.

Hoffmann, Stefan-Ludwig. "Introduction: Genealogies of Human Rights." *Human Rights in the Twentieth Century*, edited by Stefan-Ludwig Hoffmann, Cambridge UP, 2011, pp. 1-26.

Holmes, Richard, and Martin Matrix Evans, editors. *Battlefield: Decisive Conflicts in History*. Oxford UP, 2006.

Hong, Zicheng. *History of Contemporary Chinese Literature*. Translated by Michael M. Day, Brill, 2007. *ProQuest ebrary*, search.proquest.com/index.

Horng, Shu-ling. "Vietnam, Taiwan, and France—Yin Ling's Life Journey, Literature Creations, and Search for Subjects." *NTU Studies in Taiwan Literature*, vol. 8, 2010, pp. 153-96.

Hsia, Wan-Yun. "Castle and Pigeons—Yin Ling's Poems of Escape and Resistance." *Bulletin of Taiwanese Poetics*, vol. 27, May 2016, pp. 7-45.

Hsia Yu. *First Person*. Translated by Steve Bradbury, Hsia Yu, 2016.

"Hsia Yu." *Re-Base: When Experiments Become Attitude*, Taipei Contemporary Culture Lab, 2018, pp. 30-31.

Hsiao Hsiao. *The New Poetics of Space*. WanJuanLou, 2017.

Hsiao Hsiao, and Wen-Ling Luo. "Yong shengming xieshi de renxia shiren Zheng Chouyu." *Chuanqi Zheng Chouyu: Zheng Chouyu shixue lunji*, edited by Hsiao Hsiao, Bai Ling, and Wen-Ling Luo, vol. 2, WanJuanLou, 2013, pp. 1-3.

Hsiung Hung. *Guanyin pusa mohesa*. Dadi, 1997.

---. *Hsiung Hung shi ji*. Vast Plain, 2012.

---. *Hsiung Hung shi jingxuan ji·shuqing shi*. Fokuang Cultural, 2014.

"Hua Guofeng." *Columbia Electronic Encyclopedia*, 6th ed., Columbia UP, 2019. *EBSCOhost*, search. ebscohost.com/login.aspx?direct=true&db=aph&AN=134520690&lang=zh-tw&site=ehost-live.

Huang, Cunxiao. *Chengshi nüxing shehui kongjian yanjiu*. Southeast UP, 2008.

Huang, Ming-Chuan, director. *Hsiung Hung*. National Museum of Taiwan Literature, 2008, disc 1.

---, director. *Yin Ling*. National Museum of Taiwan Literature, 2007, discs 1 and 2.

Huntington, Samuel P. "The Clash of Civilizations?" *Foreign Affairs*, vol. 72, no. 3, Summer 1993, pp. 22-49.

Janssen, Ronald. "What History Cannot Write: Bei Dao and Recent Chinese Poetry." *Critical Asian Studies*, vol. 34, no. 2, 2002, pp. 259-77.

Jian, Wen-Zhi. "On the Shaping of Imagery and Construction of Space in 'Xiong Hong Poetry.'" *Kaohsiung Normal University Journal: Humanities and Arts*, vol. 30, 2011, pp. 43-64.

"Jorie Graham Wins Poetry Prize." *Harvard Magazine*, Oct. 4, 2012, harvardmagazine.com/2012/10/jorie-graham-wins-forward-poetry-prize. Accessed 14 Oct. 2016.

Jung Tzu. "Xiaoping Yin Ling de 'Fangfu qiansheng.'" *Lanxing shixue*, vol. 18, 2003, pp. 10-13.

Kaldor, Mary, Henrietta L. Moore, and Sabine Selchow, editors. *Global Civil Society 2012: Ten Years of Critical Reflection*. Palgrave Macmillan, 2012.

Karagueuzian, Catherine Sona. *"No Image There and the Gaze Remains": The Visual in the Work of Jorie Graham*, Routledge, 2005.

Karasowski, Moritz. *Frederic Chopin: His Life and Letters*. Translated by Emily Hill, 3rd ed., Greenwood, 1970.

Keohane, Robert O., and Joseph S. Nye Jr. "Globalization: What's New? What's Not? (And So What?)." *Foreign Policy*, no. 118, Spring 2000, pp. 104-19.

Kinley, David. *Civilising Globalisation: Human Rights and the Global Economy*. Cambridge UP, 2009.

Ku, Hui-Chien. *Taiwan xiandaishi de kuayu yanjiu*. BoYoung, 2016.

La Piana, Siobhan. "An Interview with Visiting Artist Bei Dao: Poet in Exile." *The Journal of the International Institute*, vol. 2, issue 1, Fall 1994, quod.lib.umich. edu/j/jii/4750978.0002.102?view=text;rgn=main.

Lafont, Cristina. "Human Rights, Sovereignty, and the Responsibility to Protect." *Critical Theory in Critical*

Times: Transforming the Global Political and Economic Order, edited by Penelope Deutscher and Cristina Lafont, Columbia UP, 2017, pp. 47-73.

Lee, Kuei-Yun, editor. "Wenxue nianbiao." *Taiwan xiandangdai zuojia yanjiu ziliao huibian*, vol. 98, Taiwan National Museum of Taiwan Literature, 2017, pp. 41-56.

---, editor. "Xiaozhuan." *Taiwan xiandangdai zuojia yanjiu ziliao huibian*, vol. 98, Taiwan National Museum of Taiwan Literature, 2017, pp. 35-36.

Lee, Tsui-Ying. "Kuayue liangzhe zhi jian—lun Zheng Chouyu qingshi 'huwenxing' tese yu zhongxifang lilun zhi quanshi." *Chuanqi Zheng Chouyu: Zheng Chouyu shixue lunji*, edited by Hsiao Hsiao, Bai Ling, and Wen-Ling Luo, vol. 4, WanJuanLou, 2013, pp. 1-28.

Lehman, David. *The State of the Art: A Chronicle of American Poetry, 1988-2014*. U of Pittsburgh P, 2015.

Li, Dian. "Paradoxy and Meaning in Bei Dao's Poetry."

Positions, vol. 15, no. 1, Spring 2007, pp. 113-36.

Li, Mong. "Cong diyiben shiji tanqi—Cheng Chou-yu yu Zeng Shumei, Luo Renling, Honghong, Lingyu tan pian." *The Modernist Poetry*, vol. 16, 1990, pp. 8-23.

Li, Qin. "On Bei Dao's Resource of Creation and Literary Spirit in His Early Poems: Centered on 'The Answer.'" *Journal of School of Chinese Language and Literature, Nanjing Normal University*, no. 3, Sept. 2015, pp. 15-22.

Liao, Hsiang-jen. "A Critical Analysis of Cheng Ch'ou-yu's *Dreaming on the Earth*." *Chuanqi Zheng Chouyu: Zheng Chouyu shixue lunji*, edited by Hsiao Hsiao, Bai Ling, and Wen-Ling Luo, vol. 2, WanJuanLou, 2013, pp. 65-82.

Lin, Neng-Shih, Tung-Fa Lin, Ming-fui Pang, and Wei-kai Liu. *Zhongguo xiandai shi*. Da Zhongguo, 1997.

Lin, Wan-yu. *Ai de 24 ze yunsuan*. 2nd ed., Unitas, 2018.

---. *Ganggang fasheng de shi* [*Things That Just Transpired*]. 1st ed., Hung-Fan, 2007.

---. *Ganggang fasheng de shi* [*Things That Just Transpired*]. 1st ed., Rye Field, 2018.

---. *Naxie shandian zhi xiang ni* [*Those Lightning Bolts Point toward You*]. Hung-Fan, 2014.

---. "Shi de mohu shi gaobai." *Wenhsun Magazine*, vol. 403, 2019, pp. 75-83.

---. "Shi de qinggan duiying he shenti fuhao." 18 Mar. 2019, National Taiwan Normal University, Taipei.

---. "Shi han ge han shijie." *YouTube*, 30 Apr. 2016, www.youtube.com/watch?v=Nb0DaE6oY2k.

---. "Zuwu." *Youth Literary*, vol. 575, 2001, pp. 90-91.

Lin, Yun-Wen. *(1990-2010) The Self of Construction and Space in Taiwanese Female Travel Writings*. 2010. National Cheng Kung U, PhD dissertation. *National Digital Library of Theses and Dissertations in Taiwan*, hdl.handle.net/11296/yb7s48.

Ling, Shing-jie. "Duanping." *Naxie shandian zhi xiang ni* [*Those Lightning Bolts Point toward You*], Hung-Fan, 2014, pp. 229-35.

Lionnet, Françoise, and Shu-mei Shih. "Introduction: Thinking through the Minor, Transnationally." *Minor Transnationalism*, edited by Françoise Lionnet and Shu-mei Shih, Duke UP, 2005, pp. 1-23.

Liu, Fang-xi. *"Hanyu wenhua gong xiangti" yu Zhongguo xinshi lunzheng,* Shandong jiaoyu, 2007.

Liu, Wai Tong. *Fucheng shumeng ren: Xianggang zuojia fangtan lu.* Joint, 2012.

Lo, Chih-cheng. "Tuijian yu." *Suoai lianxi* [*Practices of Love*], Elite, 2001, pp. 1-2.

Lowe, Lisa. *The Intimacies of Four Continents.* Duke UP, 2015.

Luo, Zhenya. *Zhongguo xiandai zhuyi shige shi lun* [*On the History of Modernist Chinese Poetry*]. Shehui kexue wenxian, 2002.

MacCabe, Colin. "An Interview with Stuart Hall, December 2007." *Critical Quarterly*, vol. 50, issue 1-2, Spring/Summer 2008, pp. 12-42.

McDougall, Bonnie S. "Bei Dao's Poetry: Revelation &

Communication." *Modern Chinese Literature*, vol. 1,
no. 2, Spring 1985, pp. 225-52.

Manning, Susan, and Andrew Taylor. Introduction: What
Is Transatlantic Literary Studies? *Transatlantic
Literary Studies: A Reader*, edited by Susan Manning
and Andrew Taylor, Johns Hopkins UP, 2007, pp. 1-
13.

Mascarenhas, Michael. "Crisis, Humanitarianism, and the
Condition of Twenty-First-Century Sovereignty."
Framing the Global: Entry Points for Research,
edited by Hilary E. Kahn, Indiana UP, 2014, pp. 296-
316.

Masson, Dominique. "Transnationalizing Feminist and
Women's Movements: Toward a Scalar Approach."
*Solidarities beyond Borders: Transnationalizing
Women's Movements*, edited by Pascale Dufour,
Dominique Masson, and Dominique Caouette, UBC,
2010, pp. 35-55.

Meichtry, Stacy, et al. "Paris Displays Defiance with Huge

Rally." *Wall Street Journal (Online)*, 21 Jul. 2019. *EBSCOhost*, www.wsj.com/articles/paris-displays-defiance-in-huge-rally-1420973912.

Meng Fan. "Langzi yishi de bianzou—du Zheng Chouyu de shi." *Chou-yu Cheng*, edited by Hsu-Hui Ting, National Museum of Taiwan Literature, 2013, pp. 199-215.

Minzhu, Han, editor. *Cries for Democracy: Writings and Speeches from the 1989 Chinese Democracy Movement*. Princeton UP, 1990.

Moran, Matthew. "Terrorism and the *Banlieues*: The *Charlie Hebdo* Attacks in Context." *Modern & Contemporary France*, vol. 25, no. 3, 2017, pp. 315-32. *EBSCOhost*, doi:10.1080/09639489.2017.1323199.

Morris, Adalaide. "The Act of the Mind: Thought Experiments in the Poetry of Jorie Graham and Leslie Scalapino." *Contemporary Poetry and Contemporary Science*, edited by Robert Crawford, Oxford

UP, 2006, pp. 146-66. *ProQuest ebrary*, site.ebrary.
com/lib/ntnulib/detail.action?docID=10271385.

Moyn, Samuel. *The Last Utopia: Human Rights in History.*
Belknap P of Harvard UP, 2010.

---. *Not Enough: Human Rights in an Unequal World.*
Belknap P of Harvard UP, 2018.

Munck, Ronaldo. *Globalization and Contestation: The
New Great Counter-Movement.* Routledge, 2007.

O'Neill, Bruce. *The Space of Boredom: Homeless in the
Slowing Global Order.* Duke UP, 2017.

"Nonino Prize 2013 Press Release." *Nonino Distillatori
S.p.A.,* 9 Jan. 2013, grappanonino.it/uploads/
attachments/Comunicati/Nonino_Prize_2013_Press_
Release.pdf. Accessed 12 Oct. 2016.

Ó Tuathail, Gearóid, Andrew Herod, and Susan M.
Roberts. "Negotiating Unruly Problematics." *An
Unruly World? Globalization, Governance and
Geography,* edited by Andrew Herod, Gearóid Ó
Tuathail, and Susan M. Roberts. Routledge, 1998, pp.
1-24.

Patton, Simon. Review of *Forms of Distance*, by Bei Dao. *Modern Chinese Literature*, vol. 9, no. 1, Spring 1995, pp. 139-45.

"Pingjian." *Xinshi sanbaishou bainian xinbian*, edited by Chang Mo and Hsiao Hsiao, vol. 2, Chiu Ko, 2017, pp. 884-86.

"Poetry Is Not a Crime: Nine Pulitzer-Winners among 150+ Literary Figures Calling for Israel to Release Palestinian Poet." *Mondoweiss*, 12 July 2016, mondoweiss.net/2016/07/pulitzer-literary-palestinian/.

Pozzana, Claudia. "Distances of Poetry: An Introduction to Bei Dao." *Positions* vol. 15, no. 1, 2007, pp. 91-111.

"Professor Bei Dao Listed Top Poet." *Newsletter*, no. 1. Centre for East Asian Studies, the *Chinese University of Hong Kong*, 17 Jan. 2017, cloud.itsc.cuhk.edu.hk/enewsasp/app/article-details.aspx/5BDF89CB98B83AC66D7B050A701640DB/.

Ramazani, Jahan. *Poetry and Its Others: News, Prayer,*

Song, and the Dialogue of Genres. U of Chicago P, 2014.

Ramet, Sabrina P. *Thinking about Yugoslavia: Scholarly Debates about the Yugoslav Breakup and the Wars in Bosnia and Kosovo*. Cambridge UP, 2005. *Cambridge Core*, www.cambridge.org/core/books/ thinking-about-yugoslavia/1F1419BB085C6AC1A6 E1B1389A1D3C2C.

"Reality and How to Put It to Poetry Take Stage at Cikada Prize Gathering." *Japan Times*, 24 Nov. 2016. *ProQuest*, search.proquest.com/docview/184287814 4?accountid=14228.

Ren, Ruwen. "Duoyuan wenhua jiafeng zhong de qipa—lun Yin Ling de shi." *Lanxing shixue*, vol. 18, 2003, pp. 1-9.

Rice, Kylan. "The Lateral Radical: On Jorie Graham." *West Branch*, no. 87, 2018, pp. 88-104. *EBSCOhost*, search.ebscohost.com/login.aspx?direct=true&db=hl h&AN=129664292&lang=zh-tw&site=ehost-live.

Roach Anleu, Sharyn. "Human Rights." *Globalization in Practice*, edited by Nigel Thrift, Adam Tickell, Steve Woolgar, and William H. Rupp, Oxford UP, 2014, pp. 249-53.

Rollins, J. B. "Hsia Yü's Translingual Transculturalism from *Memoranda* to *Pink Noise*." *Transcultural Identities in Contemporary Literature*, edited by Irene Gilsenan Nordin, Julie Hansen, and Carmen Zamorano Llena, Brill, 2013, pp. 245-66. *ProQuest Ebook Central*, search.proquest.com/legacydocview/ EBC/1581547?accountid=14228.

Ruan, Wenlüe. "Xianggang de Bei Dao guoji de shige." *Ming Pao*, 22 Nov. 2015, pp. 38-39.

Shen Mian. "Youya (ruci) de (richang) shenji—yuedu Lin Wan-yu *Naxie shandian zhixiang ni*." *Sea Star Poetry Quarterly*, vol. 16, 2015, pp. 21-23.

Skillman, Nikki. *The Lyric in the Age of the Brain*. Harvard UP, 2016.

Song, Ru-Shan. *Gehai tiaowang: Dalu dangdai wenxue*

lunji. Showwe Information, 2007.

Song, Yaoliang. *Shinian wenxue zhuchao* [*Major Literary Trends over Ten Years*]. Shanghai wenyi, 1988.

Spiegelman, Willard. "Amy Clampitt, Culture Poetry, and the Neobaroque." *The Cambridge History of American Poetry*, edited by Alfred Bendixen and Stephen Burt, Cambridge UP, 2015, pp. 1079-102.

Spring, Joel. *Corporatism, Social Control, and Cultural Domination in Education: From the Radical Right to Globalization: The Selected Works of Joel Spring.* Routledge, 2013.

Stevens, Wallace. *The Collected Poems of Wallace Stevens.* Alfred A. Knopf, 1981.

"Struga Poetry Evenings Laureate Author Bei Dao Arrives in Macedonia." *Independent.mk,* 25 Aug. 2015, www.independent.mk/articles/21353/Struga+Poetry +Evenings+Laureate+Author+Bei+Dao+Arrives+in +Macedonia.

Susen, Simon. "The Place of Space in Social and Cultural

Theory." *Routledge Handbook of Social and Cultural Theory*, edited by Anthony Elliott, Routledge, 2014, pp. 333-57.

Taiwan History Zheng Chou Yu. 12 Oct. 2014, video.iphone.gb.net/play/2014-10-12-台灣演義-現代詩巨擘-鄭愁予-taiwan-history-zheng-chou-yu/ft2FrtsdqkI.html.

Tan, Kathy-Ann. "'To Catch the World / at Pure Idea': Structures of Order and Disorder in Jorie Graham's Poetry." *Ideas of Order in Contemporary American Poetry*, edited by Diana von Finck and Oliver Scheiding, Königshausen & Neumann, 2007, pp. 97-114.

Tang, Xiaodu. "Chuangtong jiuxiang xueyuan de zhaohuang—Bei Dao fangtang lu" ["Tradition Is like the Call of Ancestry—an Interview with Bei Dao"]. *The Poem Waving*, vol. 3, 2004, pp. 68-72. *CNKI*, www.cnki.com.cn.

Timpane, John. "Words and Their Artists at the Princeton

Poetry Festival." *The Philadelphia Inquirer*, 14 Mar. 2013. *Newspaper Source*, web.b.ebscohost.com.

Ting, Hsu-Hui, editor. "Wenxue nianbiao." *Cheng Chou-yu*, National Museum of Taiwan Literature, 2013, pp. 45-70.

Trump, Donald J. "Memorandum on Establishment of the United States Space Force." *Daily Compilation of Presidential Documents*, 19 Feb. 2019, pp. 1-4. *EBSCOhost*, 0-search.ebscohost.com.opac.lib.ntnu. edu.tw/login.aspx?direct=true&db=aph&AN=13511 7737&lang=zh-tw&site=eds-live.

Tseng, Chin-feng. "The Concept of Impermanence—Life Consciousness in Zheng Chou-Yu's Poetry." *Kaohsiung Normal University Journal*, vol. 38, 2015, pp. 23-44.

Tzu Chuan. "Heliu lide fanhua—zhuanfang shiren Yin Ling." *Xue reng weining: Yin Ling wenxue lunji*, edited by Tsung-Han Yang, Showwe, 2016, pp. 235-52.

"Under the Easels in Rome." *Wall Street Journal*, 10 Feb. 2015, www.wsj.com/articles/under-the-easels-in-rome-1423587910. Accessed 15 Oct. 2016.

Velinger, Jan. "National Museum Opens Former Federal Parliament Building to the Public." *Czech Radio 7, Radio Prague*. 14 Aug. 2009, www.radio.cz/en/section/arts/national-museum-opens-former-federal-parliament-building-to-the-public.

Wai, Isabella. "Bei Dao's Theme Song." *The Explicator*, vol. 57, no. 3, Spring 1999, pp. 184-86. *Arts & Humanities Full Text*, search.ebscohost.com.

Wandering Homecoming, Zheng Chouyu at KTSF. YouTube, 4 Dec. 2013, www.youtube.com/watch?v=Uu5kFz_pHGA.

Weinberger, Eliot. "A Note on the Translation." *Unlock*. Translated by Eliot Weinberger and Iona Man-Cheong, Anvil Press Poetry, 2000, pp. 113-17.

West-Pavlov, Russell. *Space in Theory: Kristeva, Foucault, Deleuze*. Rodopi, 2009.

Williams, Robert R. "Fichte and Husserl: Life-world, the Other, and Philosophical Reflection." *Kant, Kantianism, and Idealism: The Origin of Continental Philosophy*, edited by Thomas Nenon, Acumen, 2010, pp. 131-62.

Ya Hsien. "Qingchun de fangu—Lin Wan-yu zuopin shangdu." *Ganggang fasheng de shi*, 1st ed., Hung-Fan, 2007, pp. 7-29.

Yang, Jian-Long. "Lun Yin Ling shige chuangzuo de zhuti yixiang." *Journal of Zhengzhou University*, vol. 39, no. 1, 2006, pp. 98-100.

Yang Mu. "Zheng Chouyu chuanqi." 1974. *Cheng Chou-yu shi xuanji*, Zhiwen, 2010, pp. 11-49.

Yang, Si-ping. "On Bei Dao." *Journal of Fuling Teachers College*, vol. 21, issue 6, Nov. 2005, pp. 25-32.

Yeh, Michelle. "'Monologue of a Stormy Soul': The Poetry and Poetics of Duo Duo, 1972-1988." *World Literature Today*, vol. 85, no. 2, Mar.-Apr. 2011, pp. 51-57. *Academic Search Premier*, web.b.ebscohost.

com/ehost.

---, and N. G. D. Malmqvist, editors. "Xiong Hong." *Frontier Taiwan: An Anthology of Modern Chinese Poetry*, Columbia UP, 2001, p. 245.

Yen, Chung-Cheng. "Heijian paian—Lin Wan-Yu de *Suoai lianxi.*" *The Epoch Poetry Quarterly*, vol. 132, 2002, pp. 124-26.

Yin Ling. Interview. Conducted by Sarah Yihsuan Tso, 20 Sept. 2019.

---. "Lun shige de shehuixing—jianlun qi shehui gongneng." *Taiwan Poetry Quarterly*, vol. 18, Mar. 1997, pp. 126-28.

---. "Piaopo migong yanyi." *Poetic Leap*, 11 Jun. 2016, poeticleap.moc.gov.tw/index.php/component/k2/item/6 83-2016poeticantecessor0611.

---. "A White Dove Flew Over." *Liangan nüxing shige sanshi jia.* [*Thirty Women Poets on Two Shores*], edited by Lusung Wang and Hsiao-tsun Wen, 1st ed., P.A.C., 1999, pp. 213-14.

---. *A White Dove Passing by.* Chiu Ko, 1997.

---. *Yin Ling jieju.* Showwe, 2017.

---. "Zi *Shier ren shiji* zhi jin." *The Epoch Poetry Quarterly*, vol. 155, Jun. 2008, pp. 189-93.

Ying, Li-hua. *Historical Dictionary of Modern Chinese Literature.* Scarecrow, 2010. *ProQuest ebrary*, site.ebrary.com/lib/ntnulib/detail.action?docID=1036 1477.

Zhao, Dingxin. *The Power of Tiananmen: State-Society Relations and the 1989 Beijing Student Movement.* U of Chicago P, 2001. *ProQuest ebrary*, site.ebrary. com/lib/ntnulib/detail.action?docID=10402626.

Zheng, Cong-Xiu. "Dan zhi song—jiedu Lin Wan-yu *Keneng de huami*." *Wenhsun Magazine*, vol. 309, 2011, pp. 130-31.

Zheng Chouyu is at Tunghai University. Facebook, 13 May 2017, www.facebook.com/zhengchouyu/videos/ vb.1663483197287847/1679326249036875/?type=2&t heater.

"Zheng Chouyu nianbiao." *Zheng Chouyu shi de zixuan II.* By Chou-yu Cheng, SDX Joint, 2000, pp. 270-87.

Zhong, Wen. "Bei Dao de wenben yiyi." *Southern Cultural Forum*, issue 2, 2014, pp. 74-83. *CNKI*, www.cnki.com.cn.

Zhuang, Wei-jie. "Zheng Chouyu shige de dangdaixing yiyijiqi qishi." *Taiwan Hongkong and Overseas Chinese Literature*, vol. 2, Apr. 2010, pp. 26-29.

Index